I0541506

Out of the Ashes

Ethel Watts Mumford

1ˢᵗ WORLD
LIBRARY
Literary Society

Out of the Ashes

Ethel Watts Mumford

© 1st World Library – Literary Society, 2005
PO Box 2211
Fairfield, IA 52556
www.1stworldlibrary.org
First Edition

LCCN: 2004195613

Softcover ISBN: 1-4218-0434-4
Hardcover ISBN: 1-4218-0334-8
eBook ISBN: 1-4218-0534-0

Purchase *"Out of the Ashes"*
as a traditional bound book at:
www.1stWorldLibrary.org/purchase.asp?ISBN=1-4218-0434-4

1st World Library Literary Society is a nonprofit
organization dedicated to promoting literacy by:

- Creating a free internet library accessible from any
  computer worldwide.
- Hosting writing competitions and offering book
  publishing scholarships.

**Readers interested in supporting literacy
through sponsorship, donations or
membership please contact:
literacy@1stworldlibrary.org
Check us out at: www.1stworldlibrary.ORG
and start downloading free ebooks today.**

Out of the Ashes
contributed by Tim, Ed & Rodney
in support of
1st World Library Literary Society

I

Marcus Gard sat at his library table apparently in rapt contemplation of a pair of sixteenth century bronze inkwells, strange twisted shapes, half man, half beast, bearing in their breasts twin black pools. But his thoughts were far from their grotesque beauty - centered on vast schemes of destruction and reconstruction. The room was still, so quiet, in spite of its proximity to the crowded life of Fifth Avenue, that one divined its steel construction and the doubled and trebled casing of its many windows. The walls, hung with green Genoese velvet, met a carved and coffered ceiling, and touched the upper shelf of the breast-high bookcases that lined the walls. No picture broke the simple unity of color. Here and there a Donatello bronze silhouetted a slim shape, or a Florentine portrait bust smiled with veiled meaning from the quiet shadows. The shelves were rich in books in splendid bindings, gems of ancient workmanship or modern luxury, for the Great Man had the instinct of the masterpiece.

The door opened softly, and the secretary entered, a look of uncertainty on his handsome young face. The slight sound of his footfall disturbed the master's contemplation. He looked up, relieved to be drawn for a moment from his reflection.

"What is it, Saunders?" he asked, leaning back and grasping the arms of his chair with a gesture of control familiar to him.

"Mrs. Martin Marteen is here, very anxious to see you. She let me understand it was about the Heim Vandyke. I knew you were interested, so I ventured, Mr. Gard - "

"Yes, yes - quite right. Let her come in here." He rose as he spoke, shook his cuffs, pulled down his waistcoat and ran a hand over his bald spot and silvery hair. Marcus Gard was still a handsome man. He remained standing, and, as the door reopened, advanced to meet his guest. She came forward, smiling, and, taking a white-gloved hand from her sable muff, extended it graciously.

"Very nice of you to receive me, Mr. Gard," she said, and the tone of her mellow voice was clear and decisive. "I know what a busy man you are."

"At your service." He bowed, waved her to a seat and sank once more into his favorite chair, watching her the while intently. If she had come to negotiate the sale of the Heim Vandyke, let her set forth the conditions. It was no part of his plan to show how much he coveted the picture. In the meantime she was very agreeable to look at. Her strong, regular features suggested neither youth nor age. She was of the goddess breed. Every detail of the lady's envelope was perfect - velvet and fur, a glimpse of exquisite antique lace, a sheen of pearl necklace, neither so large as to be ostentatious nor so small as to suggest economy. The Great Man's instinct of the masterpiece stirred. "What can I do for you?" he said, as she showed no further desire to explain her visit.

"I let fall a hint to Mr. Saunders," she answered - and her smile shone suddenly, giving her straight Greek features a fascinating humanity - " that I wanted to see you about the Heim Vandyke." She paused, and his eyes lit.

"Yes - portrait? A good example, I believe."

She laughed quietly. "As you very well know, Mr. Gard. But that, let me own, was merely a ruse to gain your private ear. I have nothing to do with that gem of art."

The Great Man's face fell. He was in for a bad quarter of an hour. Lady with a hard luck story - he was not unused to the type - but Mrs. Martin Marteen! He could not very well dismiss her unheard, an acquaintance of years' standing, a friend of his sister's. His curiosity was aroused. What could be the matter with the impeccable Mrs. Marteen? Perhaps she had been speculating. She read his thoughts.

"Quite wrong, Mr. Gard. I have not been drawn into the stock market. The fact is, I *have* something to sell, but it isn't a picture - autographs. You collect them, do you not? Now I have in my possession a series of autograph letters by one of the foremost men of his day; one, in fact, in whom you have the very deepest interest."

"Napoleon!" he exclaimed.

She smiled. "I have heard him so called," she answered. "I have here some photographs of the letters. They are amateur pictures - in fact, I took them myself; so you will have to pardon trifling imperfections. But

I'm sure you will see that it is a series of the first importance." From her muff she took a flat envelope, slipped off the rubber band with great deliberation, glanced at the enclosures and laid them on the table.

The Great Man's face was a study. His usual mask of indifferent superiority deserted him. The blow was so unexpected that he was for once staggered and off his guard. His hand was shaking, as with an oath he snatched up the photographs. It was his own handwriting that met his eye, and Mrs. Marteen had not exaggerated when she had designated the letters as a "series of the first importance." With the shock of recognition came doubt of his own senses. Mrs. Martin Marteen blackmailing him? Preposterous! His eyes sought the lady's face. She was quite calm and self-possessed.

"I need not point out to you, Mr. Gard, the desirability of adding these to your collection. These letters give clear information concerning the value to you of the Texas properties mentioned, which are now about to pass into the possession of your emissaries if all goes well. Of course, if these letters were placed in the hands of those most interested it would cause you to make your purchase at a vastly higher figure; it might prevent the transaction altogether. But far more important than that, they conclusively prove that your company *is* a monopoly framed in the restraint of trade - proof that will be a body blow to your defense if the threatened action of the federal authorities takes place.

"Of course," continued Mrs. Marteen, as Gard uttered a suppressed oath, "you couldn't foresee a year ago what future conditions would make the writing of those letters a very dangerous thing; otherwise you would have conducted your business by word of mouth. Believe me, I do not underrate your genius."

He laid his hands roughly upon the photographs. "I have a mind to have you arrested this instant," he snarled.

"But you won't," she added - "not while you don't know where the originals are. It means too much to you. The slightest menacing move toward me would be fatal to your interests. I don't wish you any harm, Mr. Gard; I simply want money."

In spite of his perturbation, amazement held him silent. If a shining angel with harp and halo had confronted him with a proposition to rob a church, the situation could not have astonished him more. She gave him time to recover.

"Of course you must readjust your concepts, particularly as to me. You thought me a rich woman - well, I'm not. I've about twenty-five thousand dollars left, and a few - resources. My expenses this season will be unusually heavy."

"Why this season?" He asked the question to gain time. He was thinking hard.

"My daughter Dorothy makes her debut, as perhaps you may have heard."

Gard gave another gasp. Here was a mother blackmailing the Gibraltar of finance for her little girl's coming-out party. Suddenly, quite as unexpectedly to himself as to his hearer, he burst into a peal of laughter.

"I see - I see. 'The time has come to talk of many things.'"

She met his mood. "Well, not so *much* time. You see, not *all* kings are cabbage heads - and while pigs may not have wings, riches have."

"You are versatile, Mrs. Marteen. I confess this whole interview has an 'Alice in Wonderland' quality." He was regaining his composure. "But I see you want to get down to figures. May I inquire your price?"

"Fifty thousand dollars." There was finality in her tone.

"And how soon?"

"Within the next week. You know this is a crisis in this affair - I waited for it."

"Indeed! You seem to have singular foresight."

She nodded gravely. "Yes, and unusual means of obtaining information, as it is needless for me to inform you. I am, I think, making you a very reasonable offer, Mr. Gard. You would have paid twice as much for the Vandyke."

"And how do you propose, Mrs. Marteen, to effect this little business deal without compromising either of us?" His tone was half banter, but her reply was to the point.

"I will place my twenty-five thousand with your firm, with the understanding that you are to invest for me, in

Ethel Watts Mumford

any deal you happen to be interested in - Texas, for instance. It wouldn't be surprising if my money should treble, would it? In fact, there is every reason to expect it - is there not? If all I own is invested in these securities, I would not desire them to decline, would I? I merely suggest this method," she continued, with a shrug as if to deprecate its lack of originality, "because it would be a transaction by no means unusual to you, and would attract no attention."

He looked at her grimly. "You think so?" Let me hear how you intend to carry out the rest of the transaction - the delivery of the autographs in question."

"To begin with, I will place in your hands the plates - all the photographs."

"How can I be sure?" he demanded.

"You can't, of course; but you will have to accept my assurance that I am honest. I promise to fulfill my part of the bargain - literally to the letter. You may verify and find that the series is complete. Your attorneys, to whom you wrote these, will doubtless tell you that they personally destroyed these documents, but they doubt-less have a record of the dates of letters received at this time. You can compare; they are all there; I hold out nothing."

"But if they say they have destroyed the letters - what in the name of - "

"Oh, no; they destroyed your communications perhaps, after 'contents noted.' But they never had your letters, for the simple reason that they never received them. Very excellent copies they were - most excellent."

Mr. Marcus Gard was experiencing more sensations during his chat with Mrs. Marteen than had fallen to his lot for many a long day. His tremendous power had long made his position so secure that he had met extraordinary situations with the calm of one who controls them. He had startled and held others spellbound by his own infinite foresight, resource and energy. The situation was reversed. He gazed fascinated in the fine blue eyes of another and more ruthless general.

"My dear madam, do you mean to infer that this *coup* of yours was planned and executed a year ago, when I, even I," and he thumped his deep chest, "had no idea what these letters might come to mean? Do you mean to tell me *that*?"

"Yes" - and she smiled at his evident reluctance to believe - "yes, exactly. You see, I saw what was coming - I knew the trend. I have friends at court - the Supreme Court, it happens - and I was certain that the 'little cloud no larger than a man's hand' might very well prove to contain the whirlwind; so - well, there was just a flip of accident that makes the present situation possible. But the rest was designed, I regret to admit - cold-blooded design on my part."

"With this end in view?" He tapped the photographs strewn upon his desk.

"With this end in view," she confessed.

He was silent a moment, lost in thought; then he turned upon her suddenly.

" Mind, I haven't acceded to your demands,"

Ethel Watts Mumford

he shouted.

"Is the interview at an end?" she asked, rising and adjusting the furs about her throat. "If so, I must tell you the papers are in the hands of persons who would be very much interested in their contents. If they don't see me - hearing from me won't do, you understand, for a situation is conceivable, of course, when I might be coerced into sending a message or telephoning one - if they don't *see* me personally, the packet will be opened - and eventually, after the Texas Purchase is adjusted, they will find their way into the possession of the District Attorney. I have taken every possible precaution."

"I don't doubt that in the least, madam - confound it, I don't! Now when will you put the series, lock, stock and barrel, into my hands?"

"When you've done that little turn for me in the market, Mr. Gard. You may trust me."

"On the word - of a debutante?" he demanded, with a snap of his square jaws.

For the first time she flushed, the color mantling to her temples; she was a very handsome woman.

"On the word of a debutante," she answered, and her voice was steady.

"Well, then" - he slapped the table with his open hand - "if you'll send me, to the office, what you want to invest, I'll give orders that I will personally direct that account."

"Thank you so much," she murmured, rising.

"Don't go!" he exclaimed, his request a command. "I want to talk with you. Don't you know you're the first person, man or woman, who has *held me up* - me, Marcus Gard! I don't see how you had the nerve. I don't see how you had the idea." He changed his bullying tone suddenly. "I wish - I wish you'd *talk* to me. I'm as curious as any woman."

Mrs. Martin Marteen moved toward the door.

"I'm selling you your autographs - not my auto-biography. I'm *so* glad to have seen you. Good afternoon, Mr. Gard."

She was gone, and the Great Man had not the presence of mind to escort his visitor to the door or ring for attendance. He remained standing, staring after her. His gaze shifted to the table, where, either by accident or design, the photographs remained, scattered. He chuckled grimly. Accident! Nothing was accidental with that Machiavelli in petticoats. She knew he would read those accursed lines, and realize with every sentence that in truth she was "letting him down easy." There was no danger of his backing out of his bargain. Seated at the desk, he perused his folly, and grunted with exasperation. Well, after all, what of it? He had coveted a masterpiece; now he was to have two in one - the contemplation of his own blunder, and Mrs. Marteen's criminal genius - cheap at the price. How long had this been going on? Whom had she victimized? And how in the world had she been able to obtain the whole correspondence? That his lawyers should have been deceived by copies was not so surprising - they never dreamed of a substitution; the

Ethel Watts Mumford

matter, not the letter, was proof enough to them of genuineness. But - he thumped his forehead. He had been staying with friends at Newport at the time. Had Mrs. Marteen been there? Of course! He took up the incriminating documents again and thoroughly mastered their contents, every turn of phrase, every between-the-line inference. Accidents could happen; he must be prepared for the worst. Not that negotiations would fail - but - not until the originals were in his hands and personally done away with would he feel secure. He recalled Mrs. Marteen's graceful and sumptuously clad figure, her clear-cut, beautiful head, the power of her unwavering sapphire eyes, the gentle elegance of her voice. And this woman - had - held him up!

He turned on the electric lamp, opened a secret compartment drawer in the table, abstracted a tiny key, and, deftly making a packet of the scattered proofs, unlocked a small hidden safe behind a row of first editions of Bunyan and consigned them to secure obscurity.

A moment later his secretary entered the room in response to his ring.

"I'm going out," he said. "Lock up, will you, and at any time Mrs. Marteen wants to see me admit her at once."

Mr. Saunders' face shone. He, too, was a devout worshiper at the shrine of art.

"The Vandyke?" he inquired hopefully.

"Well, no - but I'm negotiating for a very remarkable

series of letters - of - er - Napoleon - concerning - er Waterloo."

*   *   *   *   *

II

When Marcus Gard dressed that evening he was so absent-minded that his valet held forth for an hour in the servants' hall, with assurances that some mighty *coup* was toward. Not since the days of B.L. & W. or the rate war on the S. & O. had his master shown such complete absorption.

"He's like a blind drunk, or a man in a trance, he is - he's just not there in the head, and you have to walk around and dress his body, like he was a dumb wax-work. If I get the lay, Smathers, I'll tip you off. There might be something in it for us. He's due for dinner and bridge at the Met., but unless Frenchy puts him out of the motor, he won't know when he gets there" - which proved true. Three times the chauffeur respectfully advised his master of their arrival, before the wondering eyes of the club *chasseur*, before the Great Man, suddenly recalled to the present, descended from his car and was conducted to his waiting host.

The first one of the company to shake hands with him was Victor Mahr - and Victor Mahr was a friend of Mrs. Marteen. The sudden recollection of this fact made him cast such a glance of scrutiny at the gentleman as to quite discompose him.

"What's the old man up to, gimleting me in the eye like

that? He's got something up his sleeve," thought Mahr.

"I wonder did she ever corner *him*?" was the question uppermost in Gard's mind. He hated Mahr, and rather hoped that the lady had, then flushed with resentment at the thought that she would stoop to blackmail a man so obviously outside the pale. His mood was so unusual that every man in the circle was stirred with unrest and misgiving. Dinner brightened the general gloom, though there were but trifling inroads into the costly vintages. One doesn't play bridge with the Big Ones unless one's head is clear. Not till supper time did the talk drift from honors and trumps. Gard played brilliantly. His absent-mindedness changed to savage concentration. He played to win, and won.

"What's new in the art world?" inquired Denning, as he lit a cigar. "There was a rumor you were after the Heim Vandyke."

"Nothing new," Gard answered. "Haven't had time to bother. By the way, Mahr, what sort of a girl is the little debutante daughter of Mrs. Marteen - you know her, don't you?" He was watching Mahr keenly, and fancied he detected a shifty glance at the mention of the name. But Mahr answered easily:

"Dorothy? She's the season's beauty - really a stunning-looking girl. You must have seen her; she was in Denning's box with her mother at 'La Boheme' last week."

"And," added Denning, "she'll be with us again to-morrow night."

" Oh," said Card, with indifference. "The dark one - I

remember - tall - yes, she's like her mother, devilish handsome. Must send that child some flowers, I suppose."

Gard returned home, disgusted with himself. Why had he forced his mood upon these men? Why, above all things, had he mentioned Mrs. Marteen to Mahr, whom he despised? For the simple pleasure of speaking of her, of mentioning her name? Why had he suspected Mahr of being one of her victims? And why, in heaven's name, had he resented the very same notion? He lay in bed numbering the men of money and importance whom he knew shared Mrs. Marteen's acquaintance. They were numerous, both his friends and enemies. What had *they* done? What was her hold over *them*? Had she in all cases worked as silently, as thoroughly, as understandingly as she had with him? Did she always show her hand at the psychological moment? Did she rob only the rich - the guilty? Was she Robin Hood in velvet, antique lace and sables? Ah, he liked that - Mme. Robin Hood. He fell asleep at last and dreamed that he met Mrs. Marteen under the greenwood tree, and watched her as with unerring aim she sent a bolt from her bow through the heart of a running deer.

He awoke when the valet called him, and was amused with his dream. Not in years had such an interest entered his life. He rose, tubbed and breakfasted, and went, as was his wont, to his sister's sitting room.

"Well, Polly," he roared through the closed doors of her bedroom, "up late, as usual, I suppose! Well, I'm off. By the way, we aren't using the opera box next Monday night; lend it to Mrs. Marteen. That little girl of hers is coming out, you know, and we ought to do something for 'em now and again. I'll be at the library after three, if you want me."

At the office he found a courteous note thanking him for his kindness in offering to direct her investments and inclosing Mrs. Marteen's cheque for twenty-five thousand dollars. Gard studied the handwriting closely. It was firm, flowing, refined, yet daring, very straight as to alignment and spaced artistically. Good sense, good taste, nice discrimination, he commented. He smiled, tickled by a new idea. He would not give the usual orders in such matters. When a lovely lady inclosed her cheque, begging to remind him of his thoughtful suggestion (mostly mythical) at Mrs. So-and-So's dinner, he cynically deposited the slip, and wrote out another for double the amount, if he believed the lady deserving; if not, a polite note informed the sender that his firm would gladly open an account with her, and he was sure her interests "would receive the best possible attention and advice." In this case he determined to accept the responsibility exactly as it was worded, ignoring the circumstances that had forced his hand. He would make her nest egg hatch out what was required. It should be an honest transaction in spite of its questionable inception. Every dollar of that money should work overtime, for results must come quickly.

He gave his orders and laid his plans. Never had his business interests appealed to him as keenly as at that moment, and never for a moment did he doubt the honesty of the lady's villainy. She would not "hold out on him."

His first care that morning had been to make a luncheon appointment with his lawyer, and to elicit the

Ethel Watts Mumford

information that, as far as his attorney knew, the incriminating correspondence had been destroyed when received. "As soon as your instructions were carried out, Mr. Gard. Of course, none of us quite realized the changes that were coming - but - what those letters would mean now! Too much care cannot be taken. I've often thought a code might be advisable in the future, when the written word must be relied on."

Gard smiled grimly and agreed. "Those letters would make a pretty basis for blackmail, wouldn't they? Oh, by the way, you are Victor Mahr's lawyers, aren't you?"

As he had half expected, he surprised a flash of suspicion and knowledge in the other's eyes.

"What makes you speak of him in that connection?" laughed the lawyer.

"I don't," said Gard. "I happened to be playing bridge with him last night and from something he let fall I gathered your firm had been acting for him. Well, he needs the best legal advice that's to be had, or I miss my guess." He rose and took leave of his friend, entered his motor and was driven rapidly uptown.

Still his thoughts were of Mrs. Marteen, and again unaccountable annoyance possessed him. Confound it! Mahr _had_ been held up. Clifton knew about it; that argued that Mahr had taken the facts, whatever they were, to them. Had he told them who it was who threatened him? Then Clifton knew that Mrs. Marteen was a - Hang it! What possible right had he to jump to the wild conviction that Victor Mahr had been blackmailed at all? Because he was a friend of the lady's - a pretty reason that! Did men make friends of - Yes, they did; he intended to himself; why not that hound of a Mahr? Clifton *did* know something. Mahr was just the sort of scoundrel to drag in a woman's name. Why shouldn't he in such a case? Then, with one of his quick changes of mood, he laughed at himself. "I'm jealous because I think I'm not the only victim! It's time I consulted a physician. I'm going dotty. She's a wonder, though, that woman. What a brain, and what a splendid presence! But there's something vital lacking; no soul, no conscience - that's the trouble," he commented inwardly - little dreaming that he exactly voiced the criticism universally passed upon himself. Then his thoughts took a new tack. "Wonder what the daughter is like? I'll have to hunt her up. It's a joke - if it *is* on me! Must see my debutante. After all, if I'm paying, I ought to look her over. She's going to the Opera - in Denning's box - h'm!"

Gard broke two engagements, and at the appointed hour found himself wandering through the corridor back of the first tier boxes at the Metropolitan. Its bare convolutions were as resonant as a sea shell. Vast and vague murmurs of music, presages of melodies, undulated through the passages, palpitated like the living breath of Euterpe, suppressed excitement lurked in every turn, there was throb and glow in each pulsating touch of unseen instruments. Gard found his heart tightening, his nostrils expanding. A flash of the divine fire of youth leaped through his veins. Adventure suddenly beckoned him - the lure of the unknown, of the magic x of algebra in human equation. So great was his enjoyment that he savored it as one savors a dainty morsel, lingering over it, fearful that the next taste may destroy the perfect flavor.

He paced the corridor, nodding here and there, pausing for a moment to chat with this or that personage, affable, noncommittal, Chesterfieldian, handsome and distinguished in his clean, silver-touched middle age.

Inwardly he was fretting for their appearance - his debutante and Mme. Robin Hood. Of course they must do the conventional thing and be late. But to his pleased surprise, just as the overture was drawing to its close, he saw Denning and his wife approaching. Behind them he discerned the finely held head and chiseled features of the Lady of Compulsion, and close beside her a slender, girlish figure, shrouded in a silver and ermine cloak, a tinsel scarf half veiled a flower face, gentle, tremulous and inspired - a Jeanne d'Arc of high birth and luxurious rearing. Something tightened about his heart. The child's very appearance was dramatic coupled with the presence of her mother. What the one lacked, the other possessed in its clearest essence.

With a hasty greeting to Denning and his diamond-sprinkled spouse, Gard turned with real cordiality to Mrs. Marteen.

"This *is* a pleasure!" He beamed with sincerity. "Dear madam, present me to your lovely daughter. We must be friends, Miss Dorothy. Your very wise and resourceful mamma has given me many an interesting hour - more than she has ever dreamed, I believe."

He turned, accompanied them to the box and assisted the ladies with their wraps. Dorothy turned upon him a pair of violet eyes, that at the mention of her mother's name had lighted with adoration.

"Isn't she wonderful!" she murmured, casting a bashful glance at Mrs. Marteen; then she added with simple gratefulness: "I'm glad you're friends." In her child's fashion she had looked him over and approved.

A glow of pride suffused him. The obeisance of the kings of finance was not so sweet to his natural vanity. "She's one in a million," he answered heartily. "She should have been a man - and yet we would have lost much in that case - you, for instance." He turned toward Mrs. Marteen. "I congratulate you," he smiled. "She's just the sort of a girl that *should* have a good time - the very best the world can give her; the world owes it. But aren't you" - and he lowered his voice - "just a little afraid of those ecstatic eyes? Dear child, she must keep all the pink and gold illusions - " The end of his sentence he spoke really to himself. But an expression in his hearer's face brought him to sudden consciousness. Quite unexpectedly he had surprised fear in the classic marble of the goddess face. The woman, who had not hesitated to commit crime, feared the contact of the world for her child. It was a curious revelation. All that was best, most generous and kindly in his nature rose to the surface, and his smile was the rare one that endeared him to his friends. "Let her have every pleasure that comes her way," he added. "By the way, I'm sending you our box for Monday night. I hope you will avail yourself of it. My sister will join you, and perhaps you will all give me the pleasure of your company at Delmonico's afterward."

She hesitated for a moment, her eyes turning involuntarily toward the girl. Then the human dimple enriched her cheeks, and it was with real *camaraderie* that she nodded an acceptance.

His attitude was humbly grateful. "I'll ask the Dennings, too," he continued. "They're due elsewhere, I know, but they could join us."

The curtain was already rising and Gard, excusing himself, found his way to the masculine sanctuary, the directors' box, of which he rarely availed himself, and from a shadowy corner observed his debutante and her beautiful mother through his powerful opera glasses. He found himself taking a throbbing interest in the visitors at the loge opposite. He was as interested in Dorothy Marteen's admirers as any fond father could be; and yet his eyes turned with strange, fascinated jealousy to the older woman's loveliness. Suddenly he drew in the focus of his glasses. A face had come within the rim of his observation - the face of a man sitting in the row in front of him. That man, too, had his glasses turned toward the group on the other side of the diamond horseshoe, and the look on his face was not pleasant to see. A lean, triumphant smile curled his heavy purple lips, the radiating wrinkles at the corner of his eyes were drawn upward in a Mephistophelian hardness.

It was Victor Mahr. His expression suddenly changed to one of intense disgust, as a tall young man entered the Denning box and bent in evident admiration over Dorothy's smiling face. Victor Mahr rose from his seat, and with a curt nod to Gard, who feigned interest elsewhere, disappeared into the corridor.

*   *   *   *   *

III

Mrs. Marteen stood at her desk, a mammoth affair of Jacobean type, holding in her hand a sheet of crested paper, scrawled over in a large, tempestuous hand.

MY DEAR MRS. MARTEEN:

If you will be so good as to drop in at the library at five, it will give me great pleasure to go over with you the details of my stewardship. The commission with which you honored me has, I think, been well directed to an excellent result. Moreover, a little chat with you will be, as always, a real pleasure to -

Yours in all admiration,

J. MARCUS GARD.

P.S. - I suggest your coming here, as the details of business are best transacted in the quiet of a business office, and I therefore crave your presence and indulgence. -

J.M.G.

Mrs. Marteen was dressing for the street; her hands

Ethel Watts Mumford

were gloved, her sable muff swung from a gem-studded chain, her veil was nicely adjusted; yet she hesitated, her eyes upon a busy silver clock that already marked the appointed hour. The room was large, wainscoted in dark paneling; a capacious fireplace jutted far out, and was made further conspicuous by two settees of worm-eaten oak. The chairs that backed along the walls were of stalwart pattern. A collection of English silver tankards was the chief decoration, save straight hangings of Cordova leather at the windows, and a Spanish embroidery, tarnished with age, that swung beside the door. Hardly a woman's room, and yet feminine in its minor touches; the gallooned red velvet cushions of the Venetian armchair; the violets that from every available place shed their fresh perfume on the quiet air, a summer window box crowded with hyacinths, the wicker basket, home of a languishing Pekinese spaniel, tucked under one corner of the table. Mrs. Marteen continued to hesitate, and the hands of the clock to travel relentlessly.

Suddenly drawing herself erect, she walked with no uncertain tread to the right-hand wall of the mantel and pushed back a double panel of the wainscoting, revealing the muzzle of a steel safe let into the masonry of the wall. A few deft twirls opened the combination, and the metal door swung outward. Within the recess the pigeonholes were crammed with papers and morocco jewel cases. Pressing a secret spring, a second door jarred open in the left inner wall. From this receptacle she withdrew several packets of letters and a set of plates with their accompanying prints. Over them all she slipped a heavy rubber band, laid them aside and closed the hiding place with methodical care. The compromising documents disappeared within the warm hollow of her muff, and with a last glance around, Mrs. Marteen unlocked the door and descended to the street, where her walnut-brown limousine awaited her. Her face, which had been vivid with emotion, took on its accustomed mask of cold perfection, and when she was ushered into the anxiously awaiting presence of Marcus Gard, she was the same perfectly poised machine, wound up to execute a certain series of acts, that she had been on the occasion of her former visit. Of their friendly acquaintance of the last ten days there was no trace. They were two men of business met to consult upon a matter of money. The host was thoroughly disappointed. For ten days he had lost no opportunity of following up both Dorothy and her mother. Dorothy had responded with frank-hearted liking; Mrs. Marteen had suffered herself to be interested.

"How's my debutante?" he asked cordially, as Mrs. Marteen entered.

"She's very well, thank you," the marble personage replied. "I came in answer to your note."

"Rather late," he complained. "I've been waiting for you anxiously, most anxiously - but now you're here, I'm ready to forgive. Do you know, this is the first opportunity I have had, since you honored me before, of having one word in private with you?"

She ignored his remark. "I have brought the correspondence of which I spoke."

"I never doubted it, my dear lady. But before we proceed to conclude this little deal I want to ask you a question or two. Surely you will not let me languish of curiosity. I want to know - tell me - how did you ever hit upon this plan of yours?"

She unbent from her rigid attitude and answered, almost as if the words were drawn from her against her will: "After Martin, my husband died - I - I found myself poor, quite to my astonishment, and with Dorothy to support. Among his effects - " She paused and turned scarlet; she was angry at herself for answering, angry at him for daring to question her thus intimately.

"You found - " prompted Gard.

"Well - " she hesitated, and then continued boldly - "some letters from - never mind whom. They showed me that my husband had been most cruelly robbed and mistreated; men had traded upon his honor, and had ruined him. Then and there I saw my way. This man - these men - had political aspirations. Their plans were maturing. I waited. Then I 'wondered if they would care to have the matter in their opponents' hands.' The swindle would be good newspaper matter. They replied that they would 'mind very much.' I succeeded in getting back something of what Martin had been cheated out of - "

He beamed approval. "And mighty clever and plucky of you. And then?"

This time the delayed explosion of her anger came. "How dare you question me? How dare you pry into my life?"

"You dared to pry into mine, remember," he snapped.

"For a definite and established purpose," she retorted; "and let us proceed, if you will."

Gard shifted his bulk and grasped the arms of his chair.

"As you please. You deposited with me the sum of twenty-five thousand dollars. I personally took charge of that account, and invested it for you. The steps of these transactions I will ask you to follow."

"Is it necessary?"

"It is. Also that now you set before me the - autographs, together with their reproductions of every kind, on this table, and permit me to verify the collection by the list supplied by my lawyers."

She frowned, and taking the packet from its resting place, unslipped the band and spread out its contents.

"They are all there," she said slowly, and there was hurt pride in her voice.

Without stopping to consult either the memoranda or the letters, he swept the whole together, and, striding to the fireplace, consigned them to the flames.

"The plates!" she gasped, rising and following him. "They must be destroyed completely."

He smiled at her grimly. "I'll take care of that. And now, if you will come to the table, I will explain your account with my firm. I bought L.U. & Y. for you at the opening, the day following our compact, feeling sure we would get at least a five-point rise, and that would be earning a bit of interest until I could put you in on a good move. I had private information the following day in Forward Express stock. I sold for you, and bought F.E. If you have followed that market you will see what happened - a thirty-point rise. Then I drew out, cashed up and clapped the whole thing into Union Short. I had to wait three days for that, but when it came - there, look at the figures for yourself. Your account with Morley & Gard stands you in one hundred thousand dollars, and it will be more if you don't disturb the present investment for a few days."

Mrs. Marteen's eyes were wide.

"What are you doing this for?" she said calmly. "That wasn't the bargain. I'll not touch a penny more."

"Why did I do it? Because I won't have any question of blackmail between us. Like the good friend that you are, you gave me something which might otherwise have been to my hurt. On the other hand, I invested your money for you wisely, honestly, sanely and with all the best of my experience and knowledge. It's clean money there, Mrs. Marteen, and I'm ready to do as much again whenever you need it. You say you won't take it - why, it's yours. You must. I want to be friends. I don't want this thing lying between us, crossing our thoughts. If I ask you impertinent questions, which I undoubtedly shall, I want them to have the sanction of good will. I want you to know that I feel nothing but kindness for you - nothing but pleasure in your company."

He paused, confounded by the blank wall of her apparent indifference. Marcus Gard was accustomed to having his friendly offices solicited. That his overtures should be rebuffed was incredible. Moreover, he had looked for feminine softening, had expected the moist eye and quivering lip as a matter of course; it seemed the inevitable answer to that cue. It was not forthcoming. Again the conviction of some great psychic loss disturbed him.

"My dear Mr. Gard," the level, colorless voice was saying, "I fear we are quite beside the subject, are we not? I am not requesting anything. I am not putting myself under obligations to you; I trust you understand."

Had an explosion wrecked the building, without a doubt Marcus Gard, the resourceful and energetic leader of men, would, without an instant's hesitation, have headed the fire brigade. Before this moral bomb he remained silent, paralyzed, uncertain of himself and of all the world. He could not adjust himself to that angle of the situation. Mrs. Marteen somehow conveyed to his distracted senses that blackmail was a mere detail of business, and "being under obligations" a heinous crime. At that rate the number of criminals on his list was legion, and certainly appeared unconscious of the enormity of their offense. It dawned upon him that he, the Great Man, was being "put in his place"; that his highly laudable desire for righteousness was being treated as forward and rather ridiculous posing. The buccaneer had outpointed him and taken the wind out of his sails, which now flapped ignominiously. The pause due to his mental rudderlessness continued till Mrs. Marteen herself broke the silence.

"You appear to consider my attitude an inexplicable one. It is merely unexpected. I feel sure that when you have considered the matter you will see, as I do, that

Ethel Watts Mumford

business affairs must be free from any hint - of - shall we say, favoritisms?"

Gard found his voice, his temper and his curiosity at the same instant.

"No, hang it, I *don't* see!"

She looked at him with tolerance, as a mother upon an excited child.

"I have specified a certain sum as the price of certain articles. You accepted my terms. I do not ask you for a bonus. I do not ask you to take it upon yourself to rehabilitate me in your own estimation. I cannot accept this cheque, Mr. Gard, however I may appreciate your generosity." She pushed the yellow paper toward him.

The action angered him. "If," he roared, "you had obtained these by any mere chance, I might see your position. But according to your own account you obtained them by elaborate fraud, feeling sure of their eventual value; and yet you sit up and say you don't care to be reinstated in my regard - just as if money could do that - you - "

She interrupted him. "Then why this?" and she held out the statement. He was silent. "I repeat," she said, "I will not be under obligations to you or to anyone." She rose with finality, picked up the statement and cheque, crossed to the fire and dropped both the papers on the blazing logs. "If you will have the kindness to send me the purchase money, plus the sum I consigned to your keeping - as a blind to others, not to ourselves - I shall be very much indebted to you."

Gard watched her with varying emotions. "Well," he said slowly, "that money belongs to you. I made it for you and you're going to have it. In the meantime, as you may require the 'purchase money,' as you call it, to settle bills for soda water and gardenias, I'll make you out another cheque; the remainder will stay with the firm on deposit for you - whether you wish it or not. This is one time when I'm not to be dictated to - no, nor blackmailed." He spoke roughly and glanced at her quickly. Not an eyelash quivered. His voice changed. "I wish I understood you," he grumbled. "I wish I did. But perhaps that would, after all, be a great pity. You're an extraordinary woman, Mrs. Marteen. You've 'got me going,' as the college boys say - but I like you, hanged if I don't. And I repeat, at the risk of having you sneer at me again, I meant every word I said, and I still mean it; and I'm sorry you don't see it that way."

Her smile glorified her face.

"Please don't think I reject your proffered friendship," she said, extending her hand.

He would have taken it in both of his, but something in her manner warned him to meet it with the straight, firm grasp of manly assurance.

"*Au revoir, mon ami.*" She nodded and was gone.

For several moments he stood by the door that had closed after her. Then he chuckled, frowned, chuckled again and sat down once more before his work table.

*   *   *   *   *

IV

The *salons* of Mrs. Marteen's elaborate apartment were gay with flowers and palms, sweet with perfumes and throbbing with music. Dorothy, an airy, dazzling figure in white, her face radiant with innocent excitement, stood by her mother, whose marble beauty had warmed with happiness as Galatea may have thrilled to life. Everyone who was anybody crowded the rooms, laughing, gossiping, congratulating, nibbling at dainties and sipping beverages. The throng ebbed, renewed, passed from room to room, to return again for a final look at the lovely debutante and a final word with her no less attractive mother. A dozen distinguished men, both young and old, sought to ingratiate themselves, but Dorothy's joyous heart beat only for the day itself - her coming out, the launching of her little ship upon the bright waters frequented by Sirens, Argonauts and other delightful and adventurous people hitherto but shadow fictions. It was as exciting and wonderful as Christmas. She had been showered with presents, buried in roses. Everyone was filled with friendly thoughts of which she was the center. There was no envy, hatred or malice in all the world.

Marcus Gard advanced into the drawing room, the sound of his name, announced at the door, causing sudden and free passage to the center of attraction. He beamed upon Mrs. Marteen with real pleasure in her stately loveliness, and turned to Dorothy, who, her face alight with greeting, came frankly toward him. From the moment of their first meeting there had been instant understanding and liking. Gard took her outstretched hands with an almost fatherly thrill.

"You are undoubtedly a pleasing sight, Miss Marteen," he smiled; "and a long life and a merry one to you. Your daughter does you credit, dear lady," he added, turning to his hostess.

Dorothy, bubbling over with enthusiasm, claimed his hand again. "It was so sweet of you to send me that necklace in those wonderful flowers. See - I'm wearing it." She fondled a slender seed pearl rope at her throat. "Mother told me it was far too beautiful and I must send it back. But I was most undutiful. I said I wouldn't - just wouldn't. I know you picked it out for me yourself - now, didn't you?" He nodded somewhat whimsically. "There! I told mother so; and it would be rude, most rude, not to accept it - wouldn't it?"

He laughed gruffly. "It certainly would - and, really, you know your mother has a mania for refusing things. Why, I owe her - never mind, I won't tell you now - but I would have felt very much hurt, Miss Debutante, if you'd thrown back my little present. I'm sure I selected something quite modest and inconspicuous.... Dear me, I'm blocking the whole doorway. Pardon me."

He stepped back, nodding here and there to an acquaintance. Finally catching sight of his sister in the dining room, he joined her, and stood for a moment gazing at the commonplace comedy of presentations.

Ethel Watts Mumford

Miss Gard yawned. "My dear Marcus, who ever heard of you attending a tea? Really, I didn't know you knew these people so well."

Gard was glad of this opportunity. His sister had a praiseworthy manner of distributing his slightest word - of which he not infrequently took advantage.

"Well, you see, I was indebted to Marteen for a number of kindnesses in the early days, though we'd rather drifted apart before he died - had some slight business differences, in fact. But I'd like to do all I can for his widow and that really sweet child of theirs. I have a small nest egg in trust for her - some investments I advised Mrs. Marteen to make. Who is that chap who's so devoted?" he asked suddenly, switching the subject, as his quick eye noted the change of Dorothy's expression under the admiring glances of a tall young man of athletic proportions, whose face seemed strangely familiar.

Miss Gard lorgnetted. "That? Oh, that's only Teddy Mahr, Victor Mahr's son. He was a famous 'whale-back' - I think that's what they call it - on the Yale football team. They say that he's the one thing, besides himself, that the old cormorant really cares about."

Marcus Gard stiffened, and his jaw protruded with a peculiar bunching of the cheek muscles, characteristic of him in his moments of irritation. He looked again at Dorothy, absorbed in the conversation of the "whaleback" from Yale, recognized the visitor at the Denning box, and, with an untranslatable grunt, abruptly took his departure, leaving his sister to wonder over the strangeness of his actions.

Once out of the house, his anger blazed freely, and his chauffeur received a lecture on the driving and care of machines that was as undeserved as it was vigorous and emphatic.

Moved by a strange mingling of anger, curiosity and jealousy, Gard's first act on entering his library was to telephone to a well known detective agency - no surprising thing on his part, for not infrequently he made use of their services to obtain sundry details as to the movements of his opponents, and when, as often happened, cranks threatened the thorny path of wealth and prominence, he had found protection with the plain clothes men.

"Jordan," he growled over the wire, "I want Brencherly up here right away. Is he there?....All right. I want some information he may be able to give me offhand. If not - well, send him now."

He hung up the receiver and paced the room, his eyes on the rug, his hands behind his back, disgusted and angry with his own anger and disgust.

Half an hour had passed, when a young man of dapper appearance was ushered in. Gard looked up, frowning, into the mild blue eyes of the detective.

"Hello, Brencherly. Know Victor Mahr?"

"Yes," said the youth.

"Tell me about him," snapped Gard. "Sit down."

Brencherly sat. "Well, he's the head of the lumber people. Rated at six millions. Got one son, named

Theodore; went to Yale. Wife was Mary Theobald, of Cincinnati - "

Gard interrupted. "I don't want the 'who's who,' Brencherly, or I wouldn't have sent for you. I want to know the worst about him. Cut loose."

"Well, his deals haven't been square, you know. He's had two or three nasty suits against him; he's got more enemies than you can shake a stick at. His confidential lawyer is Twickenbaur, the biggest scoundrel unhung. Of course nobody knows that; Twickenbaur's reputation is too bad - Mahr goes to *your* lawyers, apparently."

"There isn't any blackmail in any of *that*," the older man snarled.

"Oh!" cried the youth, his blue eyes lighting. "Oh, it's blackmail you want! Well, the only thing that looks that way is a story that nobody has been able to substantiate. We heard it as we hear lots of things that don't get out; but there was a yarn that Mahr was a bigamist; that his first wife was living when he married Miss Theobald. She died when the boy was born, and in that case she was never his legal wife, and of course now never can be. The other woman's dead, too, they say; but who's to prove it? That would be a fine tale for the coin, if anyone had the goods to show."

"I suppose the office looked that up when they got it, didn't they? Good for the coin, eh? What did you find?"

The informant actually blushed. "You aren't accusing us, Mr. Gard!"

"Accusing nothing. I know a few things, Brencherly, remember. Baker Allen told me your office held him up good and plenty to turn in a different report when his wife employed you, and you 'got the goods on him.' Now, don't give me any bluff. I want facts, and I pay you for them, don't I? Well, when you got that story, you looked it up hard, didn't you?"

Brencherly, thoroughly cowed, nodded assent. "But we couldn't get a line on it anywhere. If there were any proofs, somebody else had them - that's all."

"U'm!" said Marcus, and sat a moment silent. When he spoke again it was with an apparent frankness that would have deceived the devil himself. "See here, I'll tell you my reason for all this, so perhaps you can answer more intelligently. Martin Marteen was a friend of mine, and I'm interested in his little daughter, who has just come out. Theodore Mahr is attentive to her, and I'm not keen about it, and what you tell me about his father doesn't make me any happier. What sort of a woman is Mrs. Marteen - from your point of view? Of course I know her well socially, but what's her rating with you?"

"Ai, sir," Brencherly answered promptly. "Exceptionally fine woman - very intelligent. I should say that, with a word from you, she ought to be able to handle the situation, and any girl living. But the boy's all right, Mr. Gard, even if Mahr isn't. And after all, there may not be a word of truth in that romance I spun to you. We couldn't land a thing. What made us think there might be something in it was that we got it second hand from an old servant of Mahr's. *He* told the man that told us; but the old boy's gone, too."

Ethel Watts Mumford

Gard rose from his chair and resumed his pacing. Brencherly remained seated, patiently waiting. Presently Gard turned on him.

"That'll do, Brencherly. You may go; and don't let me catch you tipping Mahr off that I've been having you rate him, do you understand?"

The detective sprang to his feet with alacrity. "Oh, no, Mr. Gard - never a word. You know, sir, you're one of our very best clients."

Left alone, Gard sat down wearily, ran his hands through his hair, then held his throbbing temples between his clenched fists. Somehow, on his slender evidence, that was no evidence in fact, he was convinced of the truth of Mahr's perfidy; convinced that the lady rated A1 by the keenest detective bureau in the country had obtained the proofs of guilt and used them with the same perfect business sagacity she had used in his own case. It sickened him. Somehow he could forgive her handling such a case as his. It was purely commercial; but this other was uglier stuff. His soul rebelled. He would not have it so; he would not believe - and yet he was convinced against his own logic. He had tried to cheat the arithmetic when he had tried to make her extortion money an honestly made acquisition. And she had refused to be a party to the flimsy self-deception.

Mrs. Marteen was a blackmailer, an extortioner - that was the truth, the truth that he would not let himself recognize. Her depredations probably had much wider scope than he guessed. He must save her from herself; he must somehow reach the submerged personality and awaken it to the hideousness of that other, the soulless, heartless automaton that schemed and executed crimes with mechanical exactitude. He took a long breath of determination, and again grinned at the farce he was playing for his own benefit. Through repetition he was beginning to believe in the fiction of his former intimacy with Marteen. True, he had known him slightly, had once or twice snatched a hasty luncheon in his company at one of his clubs; but far from liking each other, the two men had been fundamentally antagonistic. Neither was Dorothy an excuse for his peculiar state of mind. He was drawn to her with strong protective yearning. Her childlike beauty pleased him. He wished she were his daughter, or a little sister to pet and spoil. But it was not for her sake that he savagely longed to make the mother into something different, "remolded nearer to his heart's desire." Was it the woman herself, or her enigmatic dual personality that held him? He wished he knew. He found his mind divided, his emotions many and at cross purposes. His keen, almost clairvoyant intuition was at fault for once. It sent no sure signal through the fog of his troubled heart.

How would it all end? Ah, how would it end? He sensed the situation as one of climax. It could not quietly dissolve itself and be absorbed in the sea of time and forgotten commonplace.

As an outlet for his mental discomfort, his restless spirit busied itself in hating Victor Mahr. He had always disliked the man; now he malignantly resented his very existence; Mahr became the personification of the thing he most wished to forget - the victimizing power of the woman who had enthralled him. Gard had met the one element he could not control or change - the past ; and his conquering soul raged at its own impotence.

"There shall be no more of this!" he said aloud. "She sha'n't again. I'll - "

"I'll what?" the demon in his brain jeered at him. "What will you do? She will not 'be under obligations.' Perhaps, even, she likes her strange profession; perhaps she finds the delight of battle, that you know so well, in pitting her wits against the brains of the mighty; perhaps she has a cynic soul that finds a savage joy in running down the faults of the seemingly faultless - running them to earth and taking her profit therefrom. Who are you, Marcus Gard, to cavil at the lust of conquest - to sneer at the controlling of destinies?"

"I won't be beaten," declared his ego, "even if I have no weapon. I'll search till I find the way to the citadel, and if there is none open, I'll smash one through!"

*   *   *   *   *

V

"Mrs. Martin Marteen requests the pleasure of Mr. Marcus Gard's company at dinner" - the usual engraved invitation, with below a girlish scrawl: "You'll come, won't you? It's my very last dinner before we go South. - D."

He took a stubby quill, which, for some occult reason, he preferred for his intimate correspondence, and scribbled: "Of course, little friend. The crowned heads can wait." He tossed the envelope on the pile for special delivery, and speared the invitation on a letter file.

Two months had passed, and he was no nearer the solution of the problem he had set himself. His affection for the girl had deepened - become ratified by his experience of her sweetness and intelligence. They were "pally," as she put it, happily contented in each other's society. On the other hand, the fascination that Mrs. Marteen exercised over him was far from being placid enjoyment. She continued to vex his heart and irritate his imagination. Her tolerance of young Mahr's attentions to Dorothy drove him distracted, his only relief being that Miss Gard, his sister, swayed, as always, by his slightest wish, had developed a most maternal delight in Dorothy's presence, and was doing all in her power to make the girl's season a most successful one; also, in accord with his obvious desire - her influence was antagonistic to Mahr, his son and his motor car, his house and his flowers, everything that was his; in spite of which, Dorothy's manner toward Teddy Mahr was undoubtedly one of encouragement. Honesty compelled Gard to own that he could not find in the boy the echo of the objectionable sire. Perhaps the long dead mother, who was never a lawful wife, had, by some retributive turn of justice, endowed him wholly with her own qualities. Gard could almost find it in his breast to like the big, large-hearted, gentle boy, but for a final irony of fate - the son's blind adoration of his father, and that father's obvious but helpless dislike of the impending romance. Every element of contradiction seemed to be present in the tangle and to bind the older watchers to silence. What could anyone do or say? And meanwhile, in the pause before the storm, Dorothy's violet eyes smiled into her Teddy's brown devoted ones with tender approval.

One move only had Gard made with success, and the doing thereof had given him supreme satisfaction. The account opened in his office in Mrs. Marteen's name had been transferred to Dorothy, and with such publicity that Mrs. Marteen was unable to raise objections. Right and left he told the tale of his having desired to advise the widow of his old friend, of his successful operations, of Mrs. Marteen's refusal to accept her just gains as "too great," and his determination that the account, transferred to the daughter, should reach its proper destination. The first result of his outwitting of the beneficiary was a doubling of the usual letters inclosing a cheque and requesting advice. The secretary was plainly disgusted, but Gard grimly paid the price of his checkmate, and by his generosity certainly precluded any accusation of favoritism. As he read Dorothy's note on the invitation, he chuckled at the thought of his own cleverness, and rejoiced in the knowledge that his debutante had become somewhat his ward and protegee.

The bell of his private telephone rang - only his intimates had the number of that wire - and he raised the receiver with sudden conviction that the voice he would hear was Dorothy's. "Well, my dear?" he said. There was a little gurgle, and an obviously disguised voice replied:

"And who do you think this is?"

"Why, the queen of the debutantes, of course. I felt it in my bones; it was a pleasurable sensation."

"Wrong," the voice came back, "quite wrong. This is the superintendent of the Old Ladies' Home, and we want autographed photographs of you for all the old ladies' dressers - to cheer them up, you know."

"Certainly, my dear madam; they shall be sent at once. To your apartment, I suppose. Is there anything else?"

"Yes; you might bring them yourself. Did you know that mother has been ordered off to Bermuda at once? The doctor says she's dreadfully run down. She won't let me go with her. She wants me to do a lot of things; and then in three weeks we all go South. Mother's doctor says she mustn't wait. Isn't it a bore? And Tante Lydia is coming to-day to chaperon me. Did you get my invitation?"

Gard's heart sank. "Dear me! That's bad news. How

long will your mother be gone?"

"Oh, just the voyage and straight home again. But do come in this afternoon and have tea; perhaps you could persuade her to stay a week there - she won't obey me."

"They are very insubordinate in the Old Ladies' Home. I'll drop in this afternoon. Good-by, my dear."

He hung up the receiver and glowered. "Not well! Mrs. Marteen in the doctor's care!" He could not associate her perfection with illness of any kind. It gave him a distinct pang, and for the first time a feeling of protective tenderness. This instantly translated itself into a lavish order of violets, and a mental note to see that, her stateroom was made beautiful for her voyage.

Adding his signature to the pile of letters that Saunders handed him served to pass the moments till he could officially declare himself free for the day and be driven to the abode of the two beings who had so absorbed his interest.

He found Mrs. Marteen reclining on a *chaise-longue* in her library-sitting room, the Pekinese spaniel in her lap and Dorothy by her side. She looked weary, but not ill, and Gard felt a glow of comfort.

"Dear lady, I came at once. Dorothy advised me of your impending journey, and led me to believe you were not well. But I am reassured - you do not seem a drooping flower."

Mrs. Marteen laughed. "How 1830! Couldn't you put it into a madrigal? It really is absurd, though, sending me off like this. But they threatened me with nerves - fancy that - nerves! And never having had an attack of that sort, of course I'm terrified. I shall leave my butterfly in good hands, however. My sister is to take my place; and I sha'n't be gone long, you know."

"We hope not, don't we, Dorothy? What boat do you honor, and what date?"

Mrs. Marteen hesitated. "I'm not sure. The *Bermudian* sails this week. If I cannot go then, and that is possible, I may take the *Cecelia*, and make the Caribbean trip. It's a little longer, but on my return I would join Dorothy and Mrs. Trevor, crossing directly from Bermuda to Florida. It's absurd, isn't it, to play the invalid! But insomnia is really getting its hold on me. A good sleep would be a novelty just now, and bromides depress me, so - there you are! I suppose I must take the doctor's advice and my maid, and fly for my health's sake."

In spite of the natural tone and her apparent frankness, Gard remained unconvinced. He could not have explained why. All his life he had found his intuitions superior to his logical deductions. They had led him to his present exalted position and had kept him there. No sooner had this inner self refused to accept Mrs. Marteen's story than his mind began supplying reasons for her departure - and the very first held him spellbound. Was it another move in her perpetual game? Was she on the track of someone's secret? Was her scheming mind now following some new clew that must lead to the discovery of a hidden or forgotten crime - the burial place of some well entombed family skeleton? He shivered.

Mrs. Marteen observed him narrowly.

"Mr. Gard is cold, Dorothy. Send for the tea, dear - or will you have something else? Really, *you* look like the patient who should seek climate and rest."

"Perhaps you're right," he said slowly. "Perhaps I *will* go - perhaps with you. It would be pleasant to have your society for so many weeks, uninterrupted and almost alone. I'll think of it - if I can arrange my affairs."

He had been watching her closely, and seemed to surprise in the depths of her eyes and the slow assuming of her impenetrable manner, that his suggestion was far from receiving approval.

"But, my dear sir," she answered, "much as that would be my pleasure, would it be wise for you? Everyone tells me the next few weeks will be crucial. Your presence may be needed in Washington."

"Well, I suppose it will," he retorted almost angrily. "But I've a pretty good idea what the result will be, and my sails are trimmed."

"Then do come," she invited cordially; "it will be delightful!" She had read the meaning of his tone; knew quite as well as he that her words had brought home to him the impossibility of his leaving. She could afford to be pressing.

More and more convinced of some ulterior motive in Mrs. Marteen's departure, his irritation made him gruff. Even Dorothy, seeing his ill-temper, retired to the far corner of the room, and eyed him with surprise above her embroidery. Feeling the discord of his present mood, he rose to take his leave.

"Do arrange to come," smiled Mrs. Marteen, with just a touch of irony in her clear voice.

"You are very kind," he answered; "but, somehow, I'm not so sure you want me."

He bowed himself out and, sore-hearted, sought the crowded solitude of the Metropolitan Club. His next move was characteristic. Having got Gordon on the wire, he requested as complete a list as possible of the passengers to sail by the *Bermudian* and the *Cecelia*. A new possibility had presented itself. If the psychological moment in someone's affairs was eventuating, something for which she had long planned the denouement. That person might be sailing. If only he could accompany her, perhaps in the isolated world of a steamer's life, he might bring his will to bear - force from her a promise to cease from her pernicious activities, and an acceptance of his future aid in all financial matters - two things he had found it impossible to accomplish, or even propose, heretofore. But she was right; the moment was critical, and his presence might be necessary in Washington at any moment.

When, later that night, the lists were delivered at his home, he spent a throbbing half-hour. There were several possibilities. Mrs. Allison was Bermuda bound; so was Morgan Beresford. Both had fortunes, a whispered past and ambitions. The Honorable Fortescue, the wealthy and impeccable Senator, the shining light of "practical politics," was Havana bound on the *Cecelia*, so was Max Brutgal, the many-millioned copper baron. Mrs. Allison he discarded as a possibility. He was sure that Mme. Robin Hood would disdain such an easy victim and refuse to hound one of her own sex. Looking over the list, he singled out Brutgal, if it were the *Cecelia*, and Beresford, if it were the *Bermudian*. Beresford was devoted to the lovely and somewhat severe Mrs. Claigh. He might be more than willing to suppress some event in his patchwork past.

Gard threw the lists from him angrily. After all, what right had he to interfere? What business of his was it which fly was elected to feed the spider? He went to bed, and passed a sleepless night trying to determine, nevertheless, which was the doomed insect. He would have liked to prevent the ships from leaving the harbor, or invent a situation that would make it as impossible for Mrs. Marteen to leave as it was for him to accompany her.

A few days later, when Mrs. Marteen finally announced her intention of departing on the longer cruise, Gard seriously contemplated a copper raid that would keep Brutgal at the ticker. Then he as furiously abandoned the idea, washed his hands of the whole affair and did not go near Mrs. Marteen for three days. At the end of that time, having thoroughly punished himself, he relented, and continued to shower the lady with attentions until the very moment of her final leave taking. He accompanied her to the steamer, saw her gasp of pleasure at the bower of violets prepared for her and formally accepted the post of sub-guardian to Dorothy.

As the tugs dragged out the unwilling vessel from her berth, he caught a glimpse of Brutgal, his coarse, heavy face set off by an enormous sealskin collar, join Mrs. Marteen at the rail and bid blatantly for her attention. Gard turned his back, took Dorothy by the arm, and, in spite of her protestations, left the wharf. His motor took Tante Lydia and Dorothy to their apartment, where he left them with many assurances of his desire to be of service.

He sent a wireless message and was comforted. He wondered how, in the old days that were only yesterdays, people could have endured separation without any means of communication, and he blessed the name of Marconi as cordially as he cursed the name of Brutgal. To exasperate him further, the rest of the day seemed obsessed by Victor Mahr. He was in the elevator that took him up to his office; he was at the club in the afternoon; he was a guest at the Chamber of Commerce banquet in the evening, and was placed opposite Marcus Gard. Despite his desire to let the man alone, he could not resist the temptation to talk with him.

Mahr, whatever else he might be, was no fool, and even as Gard seemed a prey to nervous irritation, so Mahr appeared to experience a bitter pleasure in parrying his adversary's vicious thrusts and lunging at every opening in the other's arguments. Both men appeared to ease some inner turbulence, for they calmed down as the dinner progressed, and ended the evening in abstraction and silence, broken as they parted by Gard's sudden question:

"And how's that good-looking son of yours, Mahr?"

Mahr shot an underbrow glance at Gard, and took his time to answer.

"If he does what I want him to," he said at last, "he'll take a year or two out West and learn the lumber business - and I think he will."

"Good idea," said Gard curtly. "Good-night."

One day of restlessness succeeded another. Ill at ease, Gard felt himself waiting - for what? It was the strain of anxiety, such as a miner feels deep in the heart of the earth, knowing that far down the black corridor the dynamite has been placed and the fuse laid. Why was the expected explosion delayed? One must not go forward to learn. One must sit still and wait. A thousand times he asked himself the meaning of this latent dread. He set it down to his suspicions of Mrs. Marteen's departure. Then why this fibril anxiety never to be long beyond call? Surely, and the demon in his brain laughed with amusement, he did not expect her to send him a cryptic wireless - "Everything arranged; operation a success; appendix removed without opposition," or "Patient unmanageable; must use anesthetic."

Four days had passed, four miserable days, relieved only by a few pleasant hours with Dorothy and the enjoyment he always found in watching her keen delight in every entertainment. He went everywhere, where he felt sure of seeing her, and could he have removed Teddy Mahr from the obviously reserved place at Dorothy's side, he could have enjoyed those moments without the undercurrent of his troubled fears. That Mahr was rebelliously angry at the situation was evident. Gard had seen the look in his eyes on more than one occasion, and it boded evil to someone. What had he meant when he spoke of his son's probable absence of a year or more "to study the lumber business"? Gard approached the young man and found him quite innocent of any such plan.

"Oh, yes," he had answered, "father's keen on my being what he calls practical, but," and he had smiled frankly at his questioner, "I wouldn't leave now - not for the proud possession of every tree, flat or standing, this side of the Pacific."

Dorothy, when questioned, blushed and smiled and evaded, assuring Gard that of all the men she had met that season he alone came up to her ideal, and employed every artifice a woman uses between the ages of nine and ninety, when she does not want to give an answer that answers. The very character of her replies, however, convinced Gard that there was more than a passing interest in her preference. There was something sweetly ingenuous in her evasions, a softness in her violet eyes at the mention of Teddy's prosaic name that was not to be misunderstood. Gard sighed. Still the sense of impending danger oppressed him. He found himself neglectful of his many and vital interests. He took himself severely in hand, and set himself to unrelenting work, fixing his attention on the matters in hand as if he would drive a nail through them. Heavy circles appeared under his eyes, and the lines from nose to chin sharpened perceptibly. More than ever he looked the eagle, stern and remote, capable of daring the very sun in high ambitious flight, or of sudden and death-dealing descent; but deep in his heart fear had entered.

*　*　*　*　*

VI

"Hello! Oh, good morning. Is that you, Teddy?
Yes, you did wake me up - but I'm very glad. Half past
ten? - good gracious! - you never telephone me before
that? - Oh, what a whopper! You called me at half past
eight - day before yesterday - Why, of course - I know
that - but you did just the same. Why, yes, I'd love to.
What time to-morrow? That will be jolly; but do have
the wind-shield - I hate to be blown out of the car - no,
it *isn't* becoming - You're a goose! - besides, my hair
tickles my nose. No, I haven't had a word from mother,
and I don't understand it at all. She might have sent me
a wireless. Yes, I'm awfully lonely - who wouldn't
miss her? - Well, now, you don't have a chance to miss
me much - Oh, really! - I'm dreadfully sorry for you! -
poor old dear! Well, I can't, positively, to-day - to-
morrow, at three; and I'll be ready - yes, *really* ready.
Good-by."

Dorothy hung up the receiver, yawned as daintily as a
Persian kitten, rubbed her eyes and rang the maid's
bell. She smiled happily at the golden sunlight that
crept through the slit of the drawn pink curtains.
Another beautiful brand new day to play with, a day
full of delightful, adventurous surprises - a debutante's
luncheon, a matinee, a the dansant, a dinner, too.
Dorothy swung her little white feet from under the
covers and crinkled her toes delightedly ere she thrust

them in the cozy satin slippers that awaited them; a negligee to match, with little dangling bunches of blue flower buds, she threw over her shoulders with a delicate shiver, as the maid closed the window and admitted the full light of day. Hopping on one foot by way of waking up exercises, she crossed to the dressing-table, dabbed a brush at her touseled hair, then concealed it under a fluffy boudoir cap. She paused to innocently admire her reflection in the silver rimmed mirror, turning her head from side to side, the better to observe the lace frills and twisted ribbons of her coiffe. Breakfast arrived, steaming on its little white and chintz tray, and Dorothy smacked hungry lips.

"Oo - oo - how perfectly lovely - crumpets! and scrambled eggs! I'm starved!" She settled herself, eagerly cooing over the fragrant coffee. "Now, if only Mother were here," she exclaimed. "It's so lonely breakfasting without her!"

But her loneliness was not for long. An avalanche of Aunt Lydia entered the room, quite filling it with her fluttering presence. Tante Lydia's morning cap was quite as youthful as that of her niece, her flowered wrapper as belaced and befurbelowed as the lingiere could make it, and her high heeled mules were at least two sizes too small, and slapped as she walked.

"My dear," she bubbled girlishly, thrusting a stray lock of questionable gold beneath her cap, "I thought I'd just run in and sit with you. I've had my breakfast ages ago - indeed, yes - and seen the housekeeper, and ordered everything. It was shockingly late when we got in last night, my dear. I really hadn't a notion it was after three, till you came after me into the

Ethel Watts Mumford

conservatory. That *was* a delightful affair last night, I must say, even if Mrs. May *is* so loud. She isn't stingy in the way she entertains, like Mrs. Best's, where we were Wednesday. That was positively a shabby business. Now, dear, what do we do to-day? I've just looked over my calendar, and I want to see yours. Really, we are so crowded that we've got to cut something out - we really have." As she spoke she crossed to Dorothy's slim-legged, satin wood writing desk, and picked up an engagement book. "You lunch with the Wootherspoons - that's good. Then I can go to the Caldens for bridge in the afternoon at four. You won't be back from the matinee and tea at the Van Vaughns' until after six, and we dine at the Belmans' at eight. That'll do very nicely. And then, dear, about my dress at Bendel's; I do wish you could find a minute to see my fitting. I can't tell whether I ought to have that mauve so near my face, or whether it ought to be pink; and you know that fitter doesn't care *how* I look, just so she gets that gown *of* her hands, and I *can't* make up my mind - when I can't see myself at a distance *from* myself, and those fitting rooms are *so* small!"

Dorothy paused in the midst of a bite. "Tante Lydia, you *know* if she said 'mauve' you'd want 'pink' and 'mauve' if she said 'pink,' and all you really need is somebody to argue with; and, besides, they both look the same at night."

Mrs. Mellows pouted fat pink lips, and looked more than ever an elderly infant about to burst into tears.

"Dorothy," she sniffed, "I do think you are the most trying child! I only wish to look well for *your* sake. I have no vanity - why should I have? It's only my desire to be presentable on your account." Her blue orbs suffused with tears.

Dorothy leaped from the divan, to the imminent danger of the breakfast tray. "Now, Aunt Lydia, don't be foolish. I didn't mean to hurt your feelings, and, besides, you know you are the really, truly belle of the ball. Why, you bad thing! Where were you all last evening? Didn't I have to go after you - and into the conservatory, at that! And what did I find, pray - you and a beautiful white-haired beau, with a goatee! And now you say you are *only* dressing for *me* - Oh, fie! - oh, fie! - oh, fie!" She kissed her aunt on a moist blue eye, and bounced back to her seat.

The chaperon was mollified and flattered. "But, my dear," she returned to the charge, "you know mauve is so unbecoming; if one should become a trifle pale - "

Dorothy snipped a bit of toast in her aunt's direction. "But, why, my dear Lydia," she teased, "should one ever be pale? There are first aids to beauty, you know - and a very *nice* rouge can be had - "

"Dorothy, how can you!" exclaimed the lady, over-come with horror. "Rouge! What *are* you saying, and what *are* young girls coming to! At your age, I'd never heard the word, no, indeed. And, besides, my love, it is indecorous of you to address me as 'Lydia.' I am your mother's sister, remember."

Her charge giggled joyously. "Nobody would believe it, never in the world! You aren't one day older than I am, not a day. If you were, you wouldn't care whether it was mauve or pink - nor flirt in the conservatories."

" You're teasing me !" was Mrs. Mellows' belated

exclamation. "And, my dear, I don't think it *quite* nice, really."

The insistent call of the telephone arrested the conversation. Dorothy took up the receiver, and Aunt Lydia became all attention.

"Hello! - Oh, it's you again - I thought I rang off - Oh, really - no, I'm not!"

"Who is it?" questioned Aunt Lydia in a sibilant whisper.

Dorothy went on talking, carefully refraining from any mention of names. " Yes - did you? - that's awfully kind - yes, I love violets; no, they haven't come, by messenger - how extravagant! No, I'm not going out *just* yet - not in this get up. What color? Pink - *and* a lace cap - a duck of a lace cap. Send the photographs around - Oh, *that's* all right; Aunt Lydia is here - aren't you, Aunt Lydia? - Oh, oh - what a horrid word! - unsay it at once! All right, you're forgiven. I'm busy *all* day - *all, all* day - yes, and this evening. No, orchids won't go with my gown to-night - don't be silly - of course, gardenias go with everything, but - now, what nonsense! - I'm going to hang up - Indeed, I *will*. Good-b - what? Now, listen to me - "

A tap at the door, and Aunt Lydia, hypnotized as she was by the telephone conversation, had presence of mind enough to open the door and receive a square box tied with purple ribbon. She dexterously untied the loose bow knot, and withdrew from its tissue wrappings, a fragrant bouquet of violets. An envelope enclosing a card fell to the floor. With suppleness hardly to be expected from one of her years, she stooped to pick it up, and in a twinkling had the donor's name before her.

Dorothy hung up the receiver and turned. "So you know who sent the flowers, and who was on the 'phone," she laughed. "Tante, you should have been a detective - you really should."

"How can you!" almost wept Mrs. Mellows. "I only opened it to save you the trouble. Of course, I knew all along that it was Teddy Mahr - I guessed - why not? Really, Dorothy, you misinterpret my interest in you, really, you do."

Dorothy laughed. "Now, now," she scolded, "don't say that. Here, I'll divide with you." She separated the fragrant bunch into its components of smaller bunches, snipped the purple ribbon in two, and neatly devised two corsage adornments. "Here," she bubbled, "one for you and one for me - and don't say such mean things about me any more. If you do, I'll tell Mother about all your flirtations the minute she gets back - I will, too!"

"That reminds me, my dear," said Mrs. Mellows, her apple-pink face becoming suddenly serious, "I don't understand why we haven't had any news from your mother, really, I don't. She might have sent us just a wireless or something."

"It *is* odd." Dorothy's laugh broke off midway in a silvery chuckle. "But something may have gone wrong with the telegraphic apparatus, you know. We might get the company, and find out if any other messages have been received from her."

" I never thought of that," exclaimed Mrs. Mellows.

"You are quick witted, Dorothy, I will say that for you. Suppose you do find out."

Dorothy turned to the telephone and made her inquiry. "There," she said at length, "I guessed it - no messages at all; they are sure it's out of order. Well, that does relieve one's mind. It isn't because she's ill, or anything like that. Now, Aunt Lydia, that's *my* mail."

"Why, child!" the mature Cupid protested, "*I* wasn't going to open your letters. Indeed, I think you are positively insulting to me! Here, that's from your cousin Euphemia, I know her hand; and that's just a circular, I'm sure - and Tappe's bill. My dear, you've been perfectly foolish about hats this winter. This is a handwriting I don't know, but it's smart stationery - and, dear me, look at all these little cards. I really don't see how the postman bothers to see that they're all delivered; they're such little slippery things - more teas - and bridge."

"And how about yours?" questioned Dorothy, amused. "What did you get?"

Aunt Lydia bridled. "Oh, nothing much. Some cards, a bill or two - "

"Bill or coo, you mean," said her niece with a playful clutch at her chaperon's lap-full of missives. "If that isn't a man's letter, I'll eat my cap, ribbons and all - and that one, and that one."

Mrs. Mellows rose hastily, gathered her flowing negligee about her and beat a retreat.

She turned at the door, "You're a rude little girl, and I

shan't count on you to go to Bendel's. If you want me, I'll be here from half past two to four, when I go for bridge." With the air of a Christian martyr she betook herself to the seclusion of her own rooms.

Dorothy suffered herself to be dressed as she opened her mail. Aunt Lydia had diagnosed it with almost psychic exactness, and its mystery had ceased to be interesting. Last of all she opened a plain envelope with typewritten directions. The enclosure, also typewritten, gave a first impression of an announcement of a special sale, or request for assistance from some charitable organization. Idly she glanced at it, flipped it over, and found it to be unsigned. A word or two caught her attention. She turned back, and read:

Miss DOROTHY MARTEEN:

"That the sins of the parents should be visited upon the children is, perhaps, hard. But we feel it time for you to understand thoroughly your situation, in order that you may determine what your future is to be. You have been reared all your life on stolen, or what is worse, extorted money. We hope you have not inherited the callous nature of your mother, and that this information will not leave you unashamed. Not a gown you have worn, nor a possession you have enjoyed, but has been yours through theft. That you may verify this statement, open the steel safe, back of the second panel of the library wall to the left of the fireplace. The combination is, 2.2.9.6.0. A button on the inner edge on the right releases a spring, opening a second compartment, where the material of your future luxuries is stored. A look will be sufficient. I hardly think you will then care to occupy the position in the lime light to which you have been brought by such means. Obscurity is better - perhaps, even exile. Talk it over with your mother. We think she will agree with us.

The words danced before Dorothy's eyes, a sudden stopping of the heart, a hot flush, a painful dizziness that was at once physical and mental, made her clutch at the table for support. She dropped the letter, and stood staring at it, fascinated, as in a nightmare.

An anonymous letter, a cruel, hateful, wicked atrocity! Why should she receive such a thing? she, who never in her whole life, had wished anyone ill. It couldn't be so. She had misread, misunderstood. She picked up the message and looked at it again. It was surely intended for her, there could be no mistake. Then fear came upon her. The abrupt entrance of the maid, carrying her hat and veil, gave her a spasm of panic. No one must see, no one must know. The wretched sender of this hideous libel must believe it ignored - never received. She thrust the paper hastily into the bosom of her dress. Its very contact seemed to burn.

"That will do," she said. "I'm not going out just yet. I - I have some notes to write; don't bother me now."

Her voice sounded strange. She glanced quickly at the maid, fearing to surprise a look of suspicion. It seemed impossible that that cracked voice of hers would pass unnoticed. But the maid bowed, carefully placed a pair of white gloves by the hat and jacket, and went out as if nothing had happened.

Dorothy, left alone, stood still for a moment as if robbed of all volition. Then, with a suppressed cry, she dragged out the accusing document and carried it to the light. Who could do such a thing! Who would be such a lying coward! Her helplessness made her rage. Oh, to be able to confront this traducer, this libeler. To see him punished, to tell him to his face what she thought of him I Somewhere he was in the world, laughing to himself in the safety of his namelessness - knowing her futile anger and indignation - satisfied to have shamed and insulted her - and her mother - her great, resourceful, splendid mother, away and ill when this dastardly attack was made. Impulsively she turned to run to her aunt, and lay the matter before her, but paused and sat down on the little chair before her writing desk. Covering her eyes with her clenched hands she tried to think. Tante Lydia was worse than useless, scatterbrained, self-centered, incapable. What would she do? Lament and call all her friends in conclave; send in the police; acknowledge her fright, and give this nameless writer the satisfaction of knowing that his shaft had found its mark?

Teddy! Teddy would come to her at once. But what could he do? Sympathy was not what she wanted; it was support and guidance. With a trembling hand she smoothed the paper before her and, controlling herself, reread every word with minutest care. But this third perusal left her more at sea than before. What did this enmity mean? What could have incited it? Why did this wretch give her such minute instructions? She knew of no safe in the library - could it be just possible that such a thing *did* exist? Could it be possible that this liar had obtained knowledge of her mother's private affairs to such an extent that he knew of facts that had remained unknown even to her? - the daughter! A new cause for fear loomed before her. Had this venomous enemy access to the house? Was he able to come and go at will, ferreting out its secrets?

Ethel Watts Mumford

Dorothy turned about quickly, almost expecting to see some sinister shadow leering at her from the doorway, or disappearing into the wardrobe. Her terror had something in it of childish nightmare. Acting as if under a spell of compulsion, she rose and tiptoed to the door. She looked down the hall, and found it empty. The querulous voice of Mrs. Mellows came to her, raised in complaint against hooked-behind dresses. Like a lovely little ghost she flitted down the corridor to the library, paused for an instant with a beating heart, and, entering, closed the door with infinite precautions and shot the bolt.

She was panting as if from some painful exertion. Her hands were damp and chill, her temples throbbed. The room seemed strange, close shuttered and silent, as if it sheltered the silent, unresponsive dead. The air was oppressive, and the light that filtered through the dim blinds was vague and uncanny.

It was some moments before she felt herself under sufficient control to cross by the big Jacobean table, and face the hooded fireplace - "to the left, the second panel." She stared at it. To all appearances it was reassuringly the same as all the others. Gently she pushed it right and left, then up and down, but her pressure was so slight and nervous that it did not stir the heavy wood. She breathed a great sigh of relief, and beginning now to believe herself the victim of some cruel hoax, she dared a firmer pressure. The panel responded - moved - slid slowly behind its fellow - revealing the steel muzzle of a safe let into the solid masonry. It seemed the result of some evil witchcraft; her blood chilled. Yet, with renewed eagerness, she turned the combination. She did not need to refer to the letter, she knew it by heart - the numbers were seared there. The heavy door swung outward. Within she saw well-remembered cases of velvet and morocco. This contained her mother's diamond collar; that her lavalliere; the emerald pendant was in the box of ivory velvet; the earrings and the antique diamond rings in the little round-topped casket, embossed and inlaid. Sliding her finger along the inner frame of the safe, she felt a knob, and pressed it. One side of the receptacle clicked open, revealing an inner compartment.

Then panic seized her. She could never recall shutting the safe door and replacing the panel, the movements were automatic. She was out of the library and running down the corridor before she realized it. Once more in the sanctuary of her own room, she threw herself upon the bed, buried her face in the tumbled pillow and gasped for breath.

"What shall I do! - what shall I do!" she moaned aloud. "I'm afraid - Oh, I'm afraid!" like a little child crying in the night in the awful isolation of an empty house. Suddenly she sat up. The tears dried upon her curved lashes. Of course, of course - Mr. Gard, her friend, her mother's friend. The very thought of him steadied her. The terrified child of her untried self, vanished before the coming of a new and active womanhood. She thought quickly and clearly. "He would be at his office," she reasoned. "He had mentioned an important meeting. She would go there at once - cancelling her luncheon engagement on the ground of some simple ailment. Tante Lydia must not know. Once let Gard, with his master grip, control the situation, and she would feel safe as in a walled castle strongly defended. A tower of strength - a tower of strength." She repeated the words to herself as if they were a

Ethel Watts Mumford

talisman. She felt as if, from afar, her mother had counseled her. She would go to him. It was the right thing, the only thing to do.

* * * * *

VII

The morning of the fifth day since Mrs. Marteen's departure found Gard in early consultation in the directors' room of his Wall Street office, facing a board of directors with but one opinion - he must go at once to Washington. Strangely enough, the plan met with stubborn resistance from his inner self. There was every reason for his going, but he did not want to go. His advisers and fellow directors looked in amazement as they saw him hesitate, and for once the Great Man was at a loss to explain. He knew, and they knew, that there was nothing that should detain him, nothing that could by any twist be construed into a valid excuse for refusal. He amazed himself and them by abruptly rising from his seat, bunching the muscles of his jaw in evident antagonism and hurling at them his ultimatum in a voice of defiance.

"Of course, gentlemen, it is evident that I must go, and I will. The situation requires it. But I ask you to name someone else - the vice-president, and you, Corrighan - in case something arises to prevent my leaving the city."

Langley, the lawyer, rose protesting.

"But, Mr. Gard, no one *can* take your place. It's the penalty, perhaps, of being what and who you are, but the honor of your responsibilities demands it. There is more at stake than your own interests, or the interest of your friends. There's the public, your stockholders. You owe it to them and to yourself to shoulder this responsibility without any 'ifs,' 'ands' or 'buts.'"

Gard turned as if to rend him. "I have told you I'll go, haven't I? But - and there *is* a but - gentlemen, you must select another delegate, or delegation, in case circumstances arise - "

Denning's voice interrupted from the end of the table. "Gard, what excuse is the only excuse for not returning one's partner's lead? Sudden death."

"Or when you *must* have the lead yourself," snapped Gard. "I cannot go into this matter with you, gentlemen. The contingency I speak of is very remote - if it is a contingency at all. But I must be frank. I cannot have you take my enforced absence, if such should be necessary, as defalcation or a shirking of my duty - so I warn you."

"The chance is remote," Denning replied in quiet tones that palliated. "Let us decide, then, who, in case this vague possibility should shape itself, will act as delegates. I do not think we can improve on the president's suggestion, but," and he turned to Gard sternly, "I trust the contingency is *so* remote that we may consider it an impossibility for all our sakes, and your own."

Gard did not answer. In silence he heard the motion carried, and silently and without his usual affability he turned and left the room. The others eyed each other with open discomfiture.

"Well, gentlemen, the meeting is over," said Denning gloomily. "We may as well adjourn."

A very puzzled and uneasy group dispersed before the tall marble office building, while in his own private office Gard paced the floor, from time to time punching the open palm of his left hand with the clenched fist of his right, in fury at himself.

"Am I mad - am I mad?" he repeated mechanically. "Has the devil gotten into me?" His confidential clerk knocked, and seeing the Great Man's face, paused in trepidation. "What is it? What is it?" snapped Gard.

"There's Brenchcrly, sir, in the outer office. He wouldn't give his message - said you'd want to see him in private; so I ventured - "

"Brencherly!" Gard's heart missed a beat. He stopped short. He felt the mysterious dread from which he had suffered to be shaping itself from the darkness of uncertainty. "Show him in," he ordered, and, turning to the window, gazed blindly out, centering his self-control. "Well?" he said without turning, as he heard the door open and close again.

"Mr. Gard," came the quiet voice of the detective, "I've a piece of information, that, from what you told me the other day, I thought might interest you. I have found out that Mr. Mahr is making every effort to find out the combination of Mrs. Marteen's private safe."

"What!"

"Yes. I learned it from one of the men in the Cole agency. Mr. Mahr didn't come to us. I'm not betraying any trust, you see. It was Balling, one of the cleverest men they've got, but he drinks. I was out with him last night, and he let it out; he said it was the rummiest job they'd had in a long day, and that his chief wouldn't have taken it, but he had a lot of commissions from Mahr, and I guess, besides, he gave some reason for wanting it that sort of squared him. Anyhow, that's how it stands."

"Have they got it?" Gard demanded.

"No, they hadn't, but he said they expected to land it O.K. They know the make, and they've got access to the company's books, and the company's people, and if she hasn't changed the combination lately, they'll land that all right. I tried to find out if they'd put anyone into the apartment, but Balling sobered up a bit by that time and shut down on the talk. But it's dollars to doughnuts he's after something, and they've put a flattie around somewhere. Of course I don't know how this frames up with what you told me about young Mahr, but I thought you might dope it out, perhaps."

Gard sat down before his writing table, and wrote out a substantial cheque.

"There, Brencherly, that's for you. Thank you. Now I put you on this officially. Find out for me, if you can, if they have put anyone in the house. Find out what they're after. Anything at all that concerns this matter is of interest to me. Put a man to shadow Balling; have a watch put on anyone you think is acting for Mahr. I will take it upon myself to have the combination changed. I'll send a message to Mrs. Marteen."

Brencherly shook his head. " If you do that they'll

tumble to you, Mr. Gard. It's an even chance Mr. Mahr would have any messages reported. He could, you know; he's a pretty important stockholder in the transmission companies. You'd better have a watch-man or an alarm attachment on the safe, if you can."

Gard sat silent. He was reasoning out the motive of Mahr's move. Did Mrs. Marteen still retain evidence against him which he was anxious to obtain during her absence? It seemed the obvious conclusion, and yet there was the possibility that Mahr contemplated vengeance, that in the safe he hoped to obtain evidence against Mrs. Marteen herself that would put her into his hands. On the whole, that seemed the most likely explanation, and one that offered such possibilities that he ground his teeth. He was roused from his reverie by Brencherly's hesitating voice.

"I think, Mr. Gard, I'd better go at once. I want to get a trailer after Balling, and if I'm a good guesser, we haven't any time to lose."

"You're right; go on. I was thinking what precautions had best be taken at Mrs. Marteen's home. I'll plan that - you do the rest. Good-by."

Brencherly sidled to the door, bowed and disappeared.

The telephone bell on the table rang sharply. Gard took down the receiver absently, but the voice that trembled over the wire startled him like an electric shock. It was Dorothy's, but changed almost beyond recognition, a frightened, uncertain little treble.

"Is this Mr. Gard?" A sigh of relief greeted his affirmative. "Please, please, Mr. Gard, can I see you right away?"

"Where are you, Dorothy? Of course; I'm at your service always. What is it?" he asked, conscious that his own voice betrayed his agitation.

"I'm downstairs, in the building. You don't mind, do you?"

"Mind! Come up at once - or I'll send down for you."

"No - I'm coming now; thank you so much."

The receiver clicked, and Gard, anxious and puzzled, pressed the desk button for his man.

"Miss Marteen is coming. Show her in here."

A moment later Dorothy entered. Her face was pale and her eyes seemed doubled in size. She sat down in the chair he advanced for her, as if no longer able to stand erect, gave a little gasp and burst into tears.

"Dorothy, Dorothy!" begged Gard, distressed beyond measure. "Come, come, little girl, what is the matter? Tell me!"

She continued to sob, but reaching blindly for his hand, seemed to find encouragement and assurance in his firm clasp. At last she steadied herself, wiped her eyes and faced him.

"This morning," she began faintly, "a messenger brought this." From an inner pocket she took out a crumpled letter, and laid it on the table. "I didn't know what to do. Read it - read it!" she blazed. " It's too horrid - too cowardly - too wicked!"

He picked up the envelope. It was directed to Dorothy in typewritten characters. The paper was of the cheapest. He withdrew the enclosure, closely covered with typewriting, glanced over the four pages and turned to the end. Then he read through.

Gard crushed the letter in his hand in a frenzy of fury. So this - this was Mahr's objective, this the cowardly vengeance his despicable mind had evolved! He would strike his enemy through the heart of a child - he would humiliate the girl so that, with shame and horror, she would turn away from all that life held for her! He knew that if the bolt found lodgment in her heart she would consider herself a thing too low, too smirched, to face her world. The marriage, that Mahr feared and hated, would never take place. Doubtless that evidence which Mrs. Marteen had once wielded was now in his possession and with all precautions taken he was fearless of any retaliation. The obscurity and exile he suggested would be sought as the only issue from intolerable conditions. No, no, a thousand times no! Mahr had leveled his stroke at a defenseless girl, but the weapon that should parry it would be wielded by a man's strong arm, backed by all the resources of brain and wealth.

As these thoughts raced through his mind, he had been standing erect and silent, his eyes staring at the paper that crackled in his clenched fist. Dorothy's voice sounded far away repeating something. It was not till a strange hysterical note crept into her voice that he realized what she was saying.

"Speak to me, please! What shall I do? What ought I to

Ethel Watts Mumford

do? Tell me, tell me!"

"Do?" he exclaimed. "Do? Why, nothing, my dear. It's a damnable, treacherous snake-in-the-grass lie! Shake it out of your pretty head, and leave me to trace this thing and deal with the scoundrel who wrote it; and I'll promise you, my dear, that it will be such punishment as will satisfy *me* - and I am not easily satisfied."

Dorothy rose from the table. "Mr. Gard," she whispered, "you won't think badly of me, will you, if I tell you something? And you will believe it wasn't because I believed one word of that detestable thing that I did what I did - you promise me that?"

He could feel his face grow ashen, but his voice was very gentle. "What was it, my dear? Of course I know you couldn't have noticed such a vile slander. What do you want to tell me?"

"I was frightened." Dorothy raised brimming eyes to his, pleading excuse for what she felt must seem lack of faith. "I felt as if the house were filled with dangerous people. I wanted to see how much they really knew. I never heard mother speak of the safe in the library. I didn't want to speak to Tante Lydia. I - "

Gard's heart stood still. "You went to the library and located the safe - and then?"

"The combination they give is the right one - I opened it with that. Then I was so terrified that anyone - a wicked person like that - could know so much about things in our house - I slammed it shut and ran away. I could not stay in the house another minute. I felt as if I were suffocating."

The sigh that he drew was one of immeasurable relief. "Well, you are awake now, my dear, and the goblin sha'n't chase you any more. But I'm greatly troubled about what you tell me, about your having opened the safe. I want you to come with me now. Is your aunt home? Yes? Well, I'll telephone my sister to call for her and take her out somewhere. Then we'll return, and I will take all the responsibility of what I think it's best to do. One thing is quite evident: your mother's valuables are not safe, if they haven't already been tampered with and stolen. You see - well, I'll explain as we go. I'll get rid of Mrs. Mellows first."

A few telephone calls arranged matters, and a message brought his motor from its neighboring waiting place. "You see," he continued, as the machine throbbed its way northward, "there are several possibilities. One is, that this anonymous person is mad. In that case, we can't take too many precautions. The ingenuity of the insane is proverbial. Then, this may be a vicious vengeance; someone who hates your splendid mother, and would hurt her through you. You can see that if you had believed this detestable story it would have broken her heart. Now such a person, hoping that you would investigate, would have been quite capable of stocking your mother's secret compartment with stuff that at the first glance would have seemed to substantiate the story. You see, they knew all about the combination and the inner compartment, and they must have had access to your home. They probably took you for a silly little fool, full of curiosity, and counted on the shock of falling into their trap being so great that you would be in no condition to reason matters out; that you and your mother would be hopelessly estranged, or at least that you would so hurt and distress her that they could gloat over her unhappiness.

You know you are the one thing she loves in all the world, Dorothy."

He had talked looking straight ahead of him, striving to give his words judicial weight. Now he glanced down at Dorothy's face. It was calm, and a little color was returning to her cheeks. She pressed his hand fervently.

"But it's so wicked!" she repeated. "It frightens me to think of such viciousness so near to us, and we don't know and can't guess who it is."

"We'll find a clew. I'll have detectives to watch the house, and to trace the messenger who brought that letter, if possible. Say nothing to anyone, not even to Tante Lydia. Perhaps it would be best not to worry your mother at all about it. She's not well, you see. In the meantime, I'm going to take everything out of the safe, and transfer it to my own. I'll make a list. Then we'll change the combination."

"Oh, I wish I'd come to you the very first minute," sighed Dorothy. "You're such a tower of strength, and you make everything so easy and simple. I'm ashamed of my fright, and my crying like a baby. You are so good to me - I - I just love you."

For a second she rested her head on his shoulder with an abandon of childlike confidence, and his heart thrilled. His inner consciousness, however, warned him that a deeper motive than his desire to save Dorothy actuated him - he must shield the mother from the danger that had threatened the one vulnerable point in her armor of indifference, the love and respect of her child.

At the apartment, inquiry for Aunt Lydia elicited the information that the lady had that moment left in company with Miss Gard, and the two conspirators proceeded alone to the library.

Gard closed the door, drew the heavy leather curtain, and turned questioningly to Dorothy. With slow, reluctant movements she approached the wall, released the panel and exposed the front of the safe. With inexpert fingers, she set the combination and pulled back the door.

"Where is the spring?" demanded Gard. He could not bear to have her touch what might lie behind the second partition. "Here, dear, take out these jewel cases and see if they are all right." He swept the velvet and morocco boxes into her hands, and felt better as he heard their clattering fall upon the table. He paused, listening for an instant to the beating of his own heart. He pressed the spring, and with swimming eyes looked at what the shelves revealed. "Dorothy," he called, and his voice was brittle as thin glass, "take a pencil and make a list as I dictate: One package of government bonds; a sheaf of bills, marked $2,000; two small boxes, wrapped and sealed; three large envelopes, sealed; two vouchers pinned together. Have you got that? I'll take possession for the present. Make a copy of that list for me." He snapped fast the inner door, and turned as he thrust the last of the packets into an inner pocket. "Now, thank you, my dear; and how about the valuables?"

"There's nothing missing," said Dorothy, handing him a written slip, "except things I know mother took with her. So robbery wasn't the motive. I think you must be right. It's some crank. But, oh, if you only knew how afraid I am to stay here! I'm afraid of my own shadow; I'm afraid of the clock chimes; when the telephone rings I'm in a panic. Don't you think I could go away somewhere, with Tante Lydia - just go away?"

Gard grasped at the suggestion. He could be sure that she would be beyond the reach of Mahr and his poisonous vengeance until he had time to crush him once and for all.

"Yes," he nodded, "you should go away. This crank may be dangerous. We know he is cunning. You should go with your chaperon - say nothing about where to anyone, not to a soul, mind; not to the servants here, not even to Teddy Mahr. Just run down incognito to Atlantic City or Lakewood, or better still, to some little place where you are not known. Write your polite little notes, and say your first season has been too strenuous, and run away. When can you go? To-night? To-morrow morning?"

"Yes, I could be ready to-night; but what shall we say to Tante Lydia?"

"Half the truth," he answered. "I'll take the responsibility. I'll tell her I've been informed by my private people that an anonymous person has been threatening you; that they are trying to locate him; and that as he is known to be dangerous, I've advised your leaving at once and quietly. I'll tell her a few of my experiences in that line, that will make her believe that 'discretion is the better part of valor.'" He laughed bitterly. "The kind attentions I've had in the way of infernal machines and threats by telephone and letter. And I see only a few, you know. What my secretaries stop and the police get on to besides would exhaust one. It's the penalty of the limelight, my dear. But don't take this too seriously. I'll have everything in hand in a day or two. Now I'm off to put your mother's valuables in a place of safety. Let's stow those jewel cases in a handbag. Can you lend me one?" She left the room and returned presently with a traveling case, into which Gard tossed the elaborate boxes without ceremony. "I've been thinking," he said presently, "that my sister's place in Westchester is open. She goes down often for week ends. There's a train at eight that will get you in by nine-thirty, and I can telephone instructions to meet you and have everything ready. If you motored down, you see, the chauffeur would know and you must be quite incognito. It'll be dead quiet, my dear, but you need a rest, and we can keep in touch with one another so easily."

Dorothy leaned forward and gazed at him with burning eyes. "You are so good," she murmured. "Of course I'll go. I know mother would want me to - don't you think so?"

He smiled grimly. "I'm certain she would. Now here are your directions; I'll attend to all the rest. All you have to do is pack. I'll send for you." He wrote for a moment, handed Dorothy the slip and began a note of explanation for Mrs. Mellows. "There," he said, as he handed over the missive for Dorothy's approval, "that covers the case. And now, my dear, the rest is my affair, and whoever he is - may God have mercy on his soul!"

* * * * *

Ethel Watts Mumford

VIII

Early on the morning following Dorothy's hurried departure, Marcus Gard, having dismissed his valet, was finishing his dressing in the presence of Brencherly.

"I tried to get you last night," he rasped; "anyhow, you're here. What have you to report to me?"

Brencherly shook his head. "As far as I can learn, sir, there's nobody slipped in the Marteen place, sir. All the information about the safe they have they got from the manufacturers and the people who installed it - only a short time ago."

Gard frowned. "Well, I happen to know they got what they were after in the way of information. But I took the liberty of being custodian of the contents of that strong box - with Miss Marteen's permission, of course - so there is nothing more to be done in that direction. Now, have you had a man trailing Mahr? What I want is an interview with him in informal and quiet surroundings, with a view to clearing the matter up, you understand. But I'd rather not ask him for a meeting. All I know about his mode of life is: Metropolitan Club after five, usually; the Opera Monday nights. Neither of these habits will assist me in the least. I want by to-morrow a pretty good list of his engagements and a general map of his day - or perhaps you know enough now to oblige me with that information."

Brencherly cast an inquisitive look at Gard. He had never accepted Gard's explanation of his interest in Mahr's affairs.

"Well," he began slowly, "I put our men on the other end of the case - Balling, the Essex Safe Company and all that, and I went after Mahr myself. I think I can give you a fair idea of his daily life. He's at the office early - before nine, usually - and by twelve he's off, unless something unusual happens. He lunches with a club of men, as I guess you know. He goes for an hour to Tim McCurdy's, the ex-pugilist, for training. Then he's home for an hour with his secretary, going over private business and correspondence. Then he goes to the club for bridge, and in the evening he's usually out somewhere - any place that's A1 with the crowd. His son he has tied as tight to the office as any tenpenny clerk; doesn't get off till after five, and then he makes a beeline for the Marteens' or goes wherever he'll find the girl. I think - but, perhaps you know best." He paused, with one of his characteristic shuffles.

Gard noted the sign and interpreted it correctly.

"If you've got a good idea, it's worth your while," he said shortly.

Brencherly blushed as guilelessly as a girl. "Oh, it's nothing, only I think - perhaps if you want to see him alone, you might pretend some business and go to his house about the time he's there every afternoon."

"And discuss our affairs before a secretary?" sneered Gard. "You can bet Mahr'd have him in the office - I know his way."

"Well, his den is pretty near sound-proof, like yours, sir. And besides, I could arrange with Mr. Long, the secretary, to have a headache, or a bad fall, or any little thing, the day you might mention - he's a personal friend of mine."

"Well, just now I don't much care how you manage it. What I want is that interview. Is your friend, Mr. Long, a confidential secretary?"

"I don't think," said Brencherly demurely, "that Mr. Mahr is very confidential even to himself."

"Could you reach him - Mr. Long, I mean - at any time?" asked Gard - he was planning rapidly.

The detective nodded toward the telephone.

"Well," growled his employer, "could your man suggest to Mahr that he had had wind of something in Cosmopolitan Telephone? I'll see that there's a move to corroborate it by noon to-day, if Long gets in his tip early. And suggest, too, that I'm sore because he bought the Heim Vandyke; but that if he asked me to come and see it, I'd go, and he might have a chance to pump me. I happen to know that Mahr is in the telephone pool up to his eyes, and he'd do anything to get into quick communication with me. He is probably going to the club to-day, and I'll not be there - see?"

Brencherly shrugged his shoulders. "Of course, if things turn out - um - fishy, Long loses his job. But he's a good man to have well placed. I guess we could land him a berth."

Gard sickened. He could read the detective's secret satisfaction in the association of that "we" in a shady transaction. Naturally, to have a man on whom they "had something" in a place of trust might be a great asset.

"Long will be taken care of," he snapped, replacing his scarf pin for the twentieth time, and making an unspoken promise to himself to send the secretary so far away from the scene of Brencherly's activities that he would at least have a chance to begin life anew without fear of the past.

"May I?" queried Brencherly, with a jerk of his head toward the telephone.

"Rather you didn't - from here. Go out, get your man and tell me when he will tip Mahr. That means my orders in the Street. Tell him there is news of federal action. I drop out enough stock to sink the quotations a few points - it's the truth, too, hang it! But it won't get very far."

A crafty smile curled the detective's lips as he rose to go. "Very good, sir. We'll pull it off all right. I suppose the office will find you?"

"Yes," said Gard. "And I see you intend to take a flier on your inside information. Well, all I say is, don't hang on too long. Get busy now; there's no time to waste."

He rang for his valet to show the man out, descended

to the dining room, dispatched his simple breakfast and turned his face and thoughts officeward. With that move came the thought of Washington. He cast it from him angrily, yet when the swirl of business affairs closed around him he experienced a certain pleasure and relief in stemming its tides and battling with its current. True, the current was swift and boded the whirlpool, but the rage that was in him seemed to give him added strength, added foresight. At least in this struggle he was gaining, mastering the flood and directing it to his will. Would his mastery be proven in this other and more personal affair? He set his teeth and redoubled his efforts, intent on proving his own power to himself. Even as Napoleon believed in his star, Gard trusted in his luck, and it was with a smothered laugh of sardonic satisfaction that news of the first move in his campaign came over the wire.

"My man has tipped his hand," came Brencherly's voice. "The other one is more than interested - excited. Make your cast and you get a bite on your picture bait."

Gard telephoned his orders to several brokers to sell and sell quickly and make no secret of it, then returned to work with a laugh upon his lips.

Contrary to his habit he remained in his office during the luncheon hour, having a tray sent in. He was to remain invisible. Mahr would doubtless make every effort to find him by what might appear accident. Later a message, asking him to join a bridge game at the Metropolitan Club, caused him to chuckle. His would-be host was a friend of Mahr's. He answered curtly that he was sick of wasting his time at cards, and had decided to drop it for a while, hanging up the receiver so abruptly that the conversation ceased in the midst of a word. An hour later Mahr addressed him over the wire.

"Ah, Gard, is that you? I called you up to tell you the Heim Vandyke has just been sent up to me. I hear you were interested in it yourself, though you saw only the photograph. Don't you want to stop in on your way uptown and see it? It's a gem. You'll be sorry you didn't bid on it. But, joking aside, you're the connoisseur whose opinion I want. I don't give a continental about the dealers; they'll fill you up with anything." Gard growled a brief acceptance. "I'll be glad to see you. Good-by."

Abruptly he terminated his interviews and conferences, adjourning all business till the following day. Mentioning an hour when, if necessary, he might be found in his home, he dismissed his officials, slipped into his overcoat, secured his hat, turned at the door of his private office, muttering something about his stick, and, quickly crossing the room, opened a drawer of his writing table and drew forth a small, snub-nosed revolver. He hesitated a moment, tossed it back, and squaring his shoulders strode from the room.

Half an hour later he entered the spacious lobby of Victor Mahr's ostentatious dwelling.

"Mr. Mahr is expecting you, sir," said the solemn servant, who conducted him to a vast anteroom, hung with trophies of armor, and bowed him into a second room, book-lined and businesslike, evidently the secretary's private office, deserted now and in some confusion, as if the occupant had left in haste. The servant crossed to a door opposite, and having discreetly knocked and announced the distinguished visitor, bowed and retired. The lackey would have taken Gard's overcoat and hat, but he retained his hold upon them, as if determined that his stay should be short.

Mahr rose to greet him, his hand extended. Gard's impedimenta seemed to preclude the handshake, and the host hastened to insist upon his guest being relieved.

Gard shook his head. "I have only a moment to inspect your picture, Mahr," he said coldly.

"Oh, no, don't say that. Have a highball; you will find everything on the table. What can I give you? This Scotch is excellent."

"No," said Gard sternly. "Excuse me; I am here for one purpose."

Mahr was chagrined, but switched on the electric lights above the canvas occupying the place of honor on the crowded wall. The portrait stood revealed, a jewel of color, rich as a ruby, mysterious as an autumn night, vivid in its humanity, divine in its art, palpitating with life, yet remote as death itself. The marvelous canvas glowed before them - a thing to quell anger, to stifle love, to still hate itself in an impulse of admiration.

Suddenly Marcus Gard began to laugh, as he had laughed that day long ago, at his own discomfiture.

"What is it?" stuttered Mahr, amazed. "Don't you think it genuine?" There was panic in his tone.

Gard laughed again, then broke off as suddenly as he had begun; and passion thrilled in his voice as he turned fierce eyes upon his enemy.

"I am laughing at the singular role this painting has played in my life. We have met before - the Heim Vandyke and I. If Fate chooses to turn painter, we must grind his colors, I suppose. But what I intend to grind first, is you, Victor Mahr! You - you cowardly hound! No - stand where you are; don't go near that bell. It's hard enough for me to keep my hands off you as it is!"

The attack had been so unexpected that Mahr was honestly at a loss to account for it. He looked anxiously toward the door, remembered the absence of his secretary and gasped in fear. He was at the mercy of the madman. With an effort he mastered his terror.

"Don't be angry," he stammered. "Don't be annoyed with me; it's all a mistake, you know. Are you - are you feeling quite well? Do let me give you something - a - a glass of champagne, perhaps. I'll call a servant."

Gard's smile was so cruel that Mahr's worst fears were confirmed. But the torrent of accusation that burst from Gard's lips bore him down with the consciousness of the other's knowledge.

"You scoundrel!" roared the enraged man. "You squirming, poisonous snake! You would strike at a woman through her daughter, would you! You would send anonymous letters to a child about her mother! You would hire sneaks for your sneaking vileness! - coward, brute that you are! Well, I know it all - *all*, I say. And as true as I live, if ever you make one move in that direction again, I shall find it out, and I will kill you! But first I'll go to your boy, Victor Mahr, and I shall tell him: 'Your father is a criminal - a bigamist. Your mother never was his wife. Sneak and beast from first to last, he found it easier to desert and deceive. You are the nameless child of an outcast father, the whelp of a cur.' I'll say in your own words, Victor Mahr: 'Obscurity is best, perhaps, even exile.' Do you remember those words? Well, never forget them again as long as you live, or, by God, you'll have no time on earth to make your peace!"

Mahr's face was gray; his hands trembled. He looked at that moment as if the death the other threatened was already come upon him. There was a moment of silence, intense, charged with the electricity of emotions - a silence more sinister than the noise of battles. Twice Mahr attempted to speak, but no sound came from his contracted throat. Slowly he pulled himself together. A look awful, inhuman, flashed over his convulsed features. Words came at last, high, cackling and cracked, like the voice of senility.

"It's you - it's *you*!" he quavered. "So she told you everything, did she? So you and she - "

The sentence ended in a hoarse gasp, as Mahr launched himself at Gard with the spring of an animal goaded beyond endurance.

Gard was the larger man, and his wrath had been long demanding expression. They closed with a jar that rocked the electric lamp on the desk. There was a second of straining and uncertainty. Then with a jerk Gard lifted his adversary clear off his feet, and shook him, shook him with the fury of a bulldog, and as relentlessly. Then, as if the temptation to murder was more than he could longer resist, he flung him from him.

Mahr fell full length upon the heavy rug, limp and inert, yet conscious.

Gard stooped, picked up his hat and gloves from where they had fallen and turned upon his heel.

At that moment the outside door of the secretary's office opened and closed, and footsteps sounded in the room beyond.

"Get up," said Gard quietly, "unless you care to have them see you there."

The sound had acted like magic upon the prostrate man. He did not need the admonition. He had already dragged his shaking body to an upright position, ere he slowly sank down into the embrace of one of the huge armchairs.

A quick knock was followed by the appearance of Teddy Mahr. The room was in darkness save for the light on the table and the clustered radiance concentrated upon the glowing portrait, that had smiled down remote and serene upon the scene just enacted, as it had doubtless gazed upon many another as strange.

"Father!" exclaimed the boy, and as he came within the ring of light, his face showed pale and anxious.

Gard did not give him time for a reply. "Good evening," he said. "I have been admiring the Vandyke. A wonderful canvas, and one thing that your father may well be proud of."

At the sound of the voice the young man turned and advanced with an exclamation of welcome. "Mr. Gard, the very one I most wanted to see. Tell me - what is the matter? Where has Dorothy gone? I've been to the house, and either they don't know or they won't tell me. She didn't let me know. I can't understand it. For heaven's sake, tell me! Nothing is wrong, is there?"

"Why, of course, you should know, Teddy." For the first time he used the familiar term. "I quite forgot about you young people. You see, Dorothy received threatening letters from some crank, and as we weren't sure what might occur I sent her off. *Mahr, shall I tell your son?*"

He turned to where the limp figure showed huddled in the depths of red upholstery. There was a question and a threat in the measured words.

"Of course, tell him Miss Marteen's address," and in that answer there was a prayer.

"Then here." Gard wrote a few words on his card and gave it into the boy's eager hand. "Run up and see her. She's with her aunt. I can bring her home any time now, however. We've located the trouble and got the man under restraint. Good-night."

*　*　*　*　*

IX

Though the heat in the Pullman was intense the tall
woman in the first seat was heavily veiled. She had
come out from the drawing room to allow more
freedom to her maid, who was packing a dressing-case
and rolling up steamer rugs. Her fellow travelers eyed
her with curiosity. She was doubtless some great and
exclusive personage, for she had not appeared in
public, not even in the diner. She sank into the vacant
seat with an air of hopeless weariness, yet her restless
hands never ceased their groping, her slim fingers
slipped in and out, in and out of the loop of her long
neck chain, or nervously twined one with another in
endless intertouch.

The long journey north was over at last. The weary
days and nights of hurried travel. Only a moment more
and the familiar sights and sounds of the great city
would greet her once again. She was going home - to
what? Mrs. Marteen did not dare to picture the future.
Pursued, as if by the Furies themselves, she had been
driven, madly, blind with suffering, back to the scene
of disaster - to know - to know - the worst, perhaps -
but to know!

Day and night, night and day, her iron will had fought
the fever that burned in her veins. Silent, self-
controlled, she had given no sign of her suffering and

Ethel Watts Mumford

her terror, though her eyes were ringed with sleeplessness and her mouth had grown stiff with its effort to command. The tension was torture. Her heart strings were drawn to the snapping point; her mind was a bowstring never relaxed, till every fiber of her resistant body ached for relief.

At last they had arrived. At last the hollow rumble of the train in the vast echoing station warned her of her journey's end. Instinctively she gave her orders, thrusting her baggage checks into the hands of her maid.

"I'm going on at once," she said. "Attend to everything. Give me my little necessaire. I don't feel quite well, and I want to get home as quickly as possible."

She hurried away before the servant could ask a question, and was directed to the open cab stand. As she stepped in, she reeled. Trepidation took hold upon her, but with enforced calm, she seated herself, and gave the address to the starter. As the motor drew away from the great buildings, she threw back her veil for the first time, and opened a window. The rush of cool air revived her somewhat, but her heart beat spasmodically, her blood seemed a thin, unliving stream. Street after street slipped by like a panorama on a screen, familiar, yet unreal. The world, her world, had changed in its essence, in its every manifestation.

At last the taxi drew up before the door of her home - was it home still? she wondered. Her hand trembled so she could not unfasten the latch, and the chauffeur, descending from his seat, came to her assistance.

" Wait, " she said in a strangled voice. "Wait; I may

want you."

At the door of her apartment she had to pause, before she rang, to gather courage, to obtain control of her whirling brain. At last the ornate door swung inward and her butler faced her with welcoming eye.

"Mrs. Marteen! Pray pardon the undress livery! No word had been received."

She took note of the darkened rooms. Only one switch, whose glow she had seen turned on as the servant came to the door, gave light. The place was hollow and unlived in as an outworn shell.

"Miss Dorothy?" she said, striving to give her voice a natural tone.

The butler h'mmed. "Miss Dorothy has gone, Madam, with Madam's sister - since yesterday. They left no address, and said nothing about when they might be expected. Mr. Gard had been with Miss Dorothy in the afternoon."

Mrs. Marteen caught hold of the broad and solid back of a carved hall chair and stood motionless, leaning her full weight on its ancient oak for support.

"That's all right, Stevens," she said at length. "You needn't notify the other servants that I have returned - for the present. I'm going right out again. I just stopped in for some important papers I may have need of. Just light the hall and the library, will you?"

With the falling of the sword that severed her last hope a new self-possession came to her - the quiet of

Ethel Watts Mumford

despair. Her brain cleared, her fevered pulse became normal, the weariness that had racked her frame passed from her. She only asked to be alone for a little - alone with her love and her memories. She quarreled no more with Fate.

The butler preceded her, lighting the way. At the door of the library, she dismissed him with a wave of her hand. Calmly she entered and softly closed the door behind her. In the blaze of the electrics she saw every nook and corner of the room - photographically - every tone and color, every glint and gleam, but her mind fastened itself with remorseless logic to one thing only - the sliding panel. In her distracted vision it seemed to move, to slip back even as she gazed. The grain of the wood appeared to writhe, to creep up and down and ripple as if with the evil life of what lay behind. She forced herself to walk across the room to lay her weakened fingers, from which all sense of touch seemed to have withdrawn, upon that vibrating panel. The face of the safe stood revealed. Slowly with growing fear she turned the numbers of the combination and paused - she could not face the ordeal, but with the releasing of the clutch, the weight of the door caused it to open slowly, as if an invisible force drew it outward and Mrs. Marteen saw before her the empty shelves within. As if in a dream she pressed the spring, and realized that the carefully planned hiding place, was hiding place no more. She stood still with outstretched arms, as if crucified. The mute evidence of that opened door was not to be refuted. Her enemy had triumphed; her own sin had found her out. No self-pity eased the awful moments. Hot pity poured in upon her heart, but not for herself in this hour of misery - but for her daughter, for the innocent sweet soul of truth, whose faith had been shattered, whose deepest love had been betrayed, whose belief in honor had been destroyed. Where had she fled? Into whose heart had she poured the torrent of her grief and shame? Could there be one thought of love, of forgiveness? Ah, she was a mother no longer. She had sold her sacred trust. She had no rights, no privileges. She must go - go quickly, efface herself forever. That was her duty, that was the only way. Like a mortally wounded creature, she thought only of some small, cramped, sheltered corner, some lair wherein to die.

With an effort she turned from the room, closed the door, and stood uncertain where to turn. Down the corridor, at its far end, was Dorothy's room. The thought drew her. She turned the knob, found the switch, and hesitated on the thresh-hold. Should she go in? Should she, the sin-stained soul, dare profane the sanctuary, the virginal altar of the pure in heart! Yes - ah, yes! - for this last time! She was a mother still.

She entered, and cast herself on her knees by the little pink and white bed. She had no tears - the springs of relief were dried in the flame of her heart's hell. She found Dorothy's pillow, a mass of dainty embroidery and foolish frills. She laid her hot cheek on its cool linen surface. In a passion of loss she kissed each leaf and rose of its needlework garland.

Then she rose to her feet. She must go, she must disappear - now, and forever from the world that had known her. She would send one message when the time came - one message - to the one man she trusted, to the one man who would fulfill her wish - that in the years to come, his watchful care should guard her child from further harm. But that, too, must wait. She rose to her feet, and crossed to the dressing-table. There was

Dorothy's picture - her little girl's picture, the one she preferred to all the others. She slipped it from its silver frame, and clasped it to her breast. She could not bear to look upon the room as she left it. She turned off the light, and crept away like a thief. She was trembling now. The calmness that had been hers as she heard her death sentence, was gone. Her overtaxed body and mind rebelled. It was with difficulty that she made her way through the deserted rooms and stumbled to the street and the waiting cab.

"Where to?" the chauffeur asked.

She gave the name of one of the large hotels. Yes, once in some such caravanserai, she might elude all pursuit. In one door and out of another - and who was to find her trace in the seething mass of the city's life? The simple transaction of paying her fare, and entering the hotel became strangely difficult. Words eluded her, she was conscious that the chauffeur eyed her oddly as he handed her her bag.

Then came a blank. She found herself once more out-of-doors, in an unfamiliar cross street. She saw a number on a lamppost, and realized that she had walked many blocks. She imagined that she was pursued - someone was lurking behind her in the shadow of an area - someone had peeped at her from behind drawn blinds. She started to run, but her bursting heart restrained her. She tried to still its beating; it seemed loud, clamorous as a drum; everyone must hear it and wonder what consciousness of guilt could make a heart beat so loudly in one's breast. She began walking again as rapidly as she dared. She must not attract attention. She must not let the shadows that followed her know that she feared them. If they guessed her panic they would lurk no longer; they would crowd close, rush upon her in vaporous throngs, stifling her like hot smoke.

She paused for breath in her painful flight. The glare from the entrance of a moving picture show fell upon her. Somehow, in that light she felt safe. The shadows could not cross its yellow glare. She breathed more easily for a moment, then became tense. A man was coming out of the white and gold ginger-bread entrance, like a maggot from some huge cake. The man was small, middle-aged, dark, with unwieldy movements and evil, predatory eyes - "Like Victor Mahr!" she said aloud; "like Victor Mahr!" The man passed before her and was gone from the circle of light into the darkness of the outer street. She gave a gasp, and her mad eyes dilated. The suggestion had gripped her. Sudden furious hate entered her soul. Victor Mahr - her enemy! The cause of all her heart break. She had forgotten how or why this was the case; but she knew herself the victim - he, the torturer. She wanted vengeance, she wanted relief from her own torment. It was he who held the key to the whole trouble. She must find him out. She must tear it from him. She strove to think clearly, to remember where she might find him. She started walking again; standing still would not find him, that was certain. Unconsciously she followed the directions her subconscious mind offered. As she walked, there came a sense of approval. She was on the right track now. Her footfalls became less dragging and aimless. She was going somewhere - to a definite place, where she would find something vastly necessary, imperative to her very life.

She neared a church; passed it. Yes, that was right. It was a landmark on her road. A white archway loomed before her in the gloom. Her journey's end - her journey's end! With that realization fatigue mastered her. She must rest before making any further effort, or she could not accomplish anything. Her limbs refused to do her bidding. The weight of her traveling case had become a crushing burden. But before she rested she must find something important that she had come so far to see - a house, a large house - what house?

She looked about her at the stately mansions fronting the square. Then recognition leaped into her eyes, and she sank upon a bench facing the familiar entrance. Now she could afford to wait. Her enemy could not escape while she sat watching. He - could - not - escape -

* * * * *

X

As Marcus Gard stood upon the steps of Mahr's residence, and heard the soft closing of its door behind him, he shut his eyes, drew himself erect and breathed deep of the keen, cold air. A rush of youth expanded every vein and artery. He experienced the physical and mental exultation of the strong man who has met and conquered his enemy. The mere personal expression of his anger had relieved him. He felt strong, alert, almost happy. He descended to the street and turned his steps homeward. At last something was accomplished. The serpent's fangs were drawn. He experienced a cynical amusement in the thought that the path of true love had been smoothed by such equivocal means. Neither of the children would ever know of the shadows that had gathered so closely around them.

But, Mrs. Marteen - what of her? Again the longing came upon him - to know her awake to herself and to her own soul; to know the predatory instinct forever quieted, that upsurging of some remote inconscience of the race's history of rapine in the open, and acquisition by stealth, forever conquered; to know her spirit triumphant. The momentary joy of successful battle passed, leaving him deeply troubled. All his fears returned. The sense of impending disaster, that had withdrawn for the moment, overwhelmed him once more.

Ethel Watts Mumford

He entered his own home absently, listened, abstracted, to the various items Saunders thought important enough to mention, dismissed him, and turned wearily to a pile of personal mail. His eye caught a familiar handwriting on a thick envelope.

From Mrs. Marteen evidently - postmarked St. Augustine. He broke the seal, wondering how her letter came to bear that mark. What change had been made in her plans? He hesitated, panic-stricken, like a woman before an unexpected telegram. He withdrew the enclosure, noting at a glance a variety of papers - the appearance of a diary.

"Dear, dear friend," it began, "I must write - I must, and to you, because you know - you know, and yet you have made me your friend - to you, because you love my little girl. They are killing me, killing me through her. I'm coming home, as fast as I can; I don't yet know how, for I'm heading the other way, and I can't stop the steamer, but I'm coming. I received a message, the second day out. It had been given to the purser for delivery and marked with the date - that's nothing unusual; I've had steamer letters delivered, one each day, during a whole crossing. I never gave it a thought when he handed it to me, I never divined. It seems to me now that I should have sensed it. I read it, and - but how to tell you? I have it here; I'll send it to you."

A sheet of notepaper was pinned to the letter. Sick at heart, Gard unfastened it. Mahr's name appeared at the bottom. Gard read: "Dear lady, you forgot to give your daughter the combination of the jewel safe and its inner compartment before you sailed. I am attending to that for you, and have no doubt that she will at once inventory the contents. We are always glad to return favors conferred upon us."

Gard's heart stood still. A sweeping regret invaded him that he had not slain the man when his hands were upon him. He threw the note aside and turned again to Mrs. Marteen's letter.

"You see," he read, "there is nothing for me to do. A wireless to Dorothy? She has doubtless had the information since the hour of my departure. What can I do? I have thought of you; but how make you, who know nothing of Victor Mahr, understand anything in a message that would not reveal all to everyone who must aid in its transmission? That at least mustn't happen. I am praying every minute that she will go to you - you, who know and have tolerated me. I can't bear for her to know - I can't - it's killing me! My heart contracts and stops when I think of it."

Further down the page, in another ink, evidently written later, was a single note:

"I've left a message with the wireless operator, a sort of desperate hope that it may be of some use - to Dorothy, telling her to consult you on all matters of importance. I've written one to you, telling you to find her. The man says he'll send them out as soon as he gets into touch with anyone."

A still later entry:

"Two P.M. - I'm in my cabin all the time. I think that I shall go mad. That sounds conventional, doesn't it - reminiscent of melodrama! I assure you it's worse than real. I feel as if for years and years I've been asleep, and now've wakened up into a nightmare. I *can* write to you; that's the one thing that gives me relief. Your kindness seems a shield behind which I can crawl. I can't sleep; I can only - not think - no, it isn't thinking I do - it's realizing - and everything is terrible. The sunlight makes ripples on my cabin ceiling; they weave and part and wrinkle. I try to fix my attention on them, and hypnotize myself into lethargy. Sometimes I almost succeed, and then I begin realizing again. And in the night I stare at the electric light till my eyes ache, and try to numb my thoughts. Must my little girl know what I am? Can't that be averted? I know it can't - I know, and yet I pray and pray - I - *pray!*"

Another sheet, evidently torn from a pad: "The wireless is out of order; they couldn't send my messages. You don't know the despair that has taken hold of me. My mind feels white - that's the only way I can describe it - cold and white - frozen, a blank. My body is that way, too. I hold my hands to the light, and it doesn't seem as if there was even the faintest red. They are the hands of a dead person - I wish they were! But I must know - must know. We are due in Havana to-morrow. I shall take the first boat out - to anywhere, where I can get a train, that's the quickest. Oh, you, who have so often told me I must stop and think and realize things! Did you know what it *was* you wanted me to do? Have you any idea what torture *is?* You couldn't! I don't believe even Mahr would have done this to me - if he had known; nobody could - nobody could. Now, all sorts of things are assailing me; not only the horror that Dorothy should *know*, but the horror of having *done* such things. I can't feel that it was I; it must have been somebody else. Why, I couldn't have; it's impossible; and yet I did, I did, I did! Sometimes I laugh, and then I am frightened at my-self - I did it just then; it was at the thought that here am I, *writing letters* - I, who have always thought letters that incriminate were the weakness of fools, the blind spot of intelligence - I, who have profited by letters - written in anger, in love, in the passion of money-getting - everything - I'm writing - writing from my bursting heart. Ah, you wanted me to realize; I'm fulfilling your wish. Oh, good, kind soul that you are, forgive me! I'm clinging to the thought of you to save me; I'm trusting in you blindly. It's five days since I left."

The sheet that followed was on beflagged yachting paper:

"What luck! I happened on the Detmores the moment I landed. They were just sailing. I transferred to them. I'm on board and homeward bound. We reach St. Augustine to-morrow night; then I'm coming through as fast as I can. I've thought it all over now. Since the wireless messages weren't sent, I shall send no cable or telegram. I shall find out what the situation is, and perhaps it will be better for me just to disappear. It may be best that Dorothy shall never see me again. I shall go straight home. I'm posting this in St. Augustine; it will probably go on the same train with me. When you receive this and have read it, come to me. I shall need you, I know - but perhaps you won't care to; perhaps you won't want to be mixed up in an affair that may already be the talk of the town. It's one thing to know a criminal who goes unquestioned and another to befriend one revealed and convicted. Don't come, then. I am at the very end of my endurance now. What sort of a wreck will walk into that disgraced home of mine? And still I pray and pray - "

Gard stood up. A sudden dizziness seized him. Go to

her! Of course he must, at once, at once; there was not a moment to be lost. He calculated the length of time the letter had taken to reach him since its delivery in the city - hours at least. And she had returned home to find - what? He almost cried out in his anguish - to find Dorothy gone, no one at the house knew where. What must she think?

He snatched up the telephone and called her number, his voice shaking in spite of his effort to control it.

The butler answered. Yes; madam had returned suddenly; had gone to the library for something; had asked for Miss Dorothy, and when she heard she was away, had made no comment, and left shortly afterwards. Yes, she appeared ill, very ill.

"I'm coming over," Gard cut in. "I'll be there in a few minutes."

He rang, ordered the servant to stop the first taxi, seized his coat and hat, left a peremptory order to his physician not to be beyond call, tumbled into his outer garments and made for the street. The taxi sputtered at the curb, but just as he dashed down the steps a limousine drew up, and Denning sprang from its opened door. His hand fell heavily upon Gard's shoulder as he stooped to enter the cab. Gard turned, his overwrought nerves stinging with the shock of the other's restraining touch.

Denning's hand fell, for the face of his friend was distorted beyond recognition. The words his lips had framed to speak died upon his tongue, as with a furious heave Gard shook him off, entered the cab and slammed the door. Denning stood for a moment surprised into inaction, then, with an order to follow, he leaped into his own car and started in pursuit.

When Gard reached the familiar entrance, his anxiety had grown, like physical pain, almost to the point where human endurance ceases and becomes brute suffering. He felt cornered and helpless. At the door of Mrs. Marteen's apartment a sort of unreasoning rage filled him. To ring; the bell seemed a futility; he wanted to break in the painted glass and batter down the door. The calm expression of the butler who answered his summons was like a personal insult. Were they all mad that they did not realize?

"Where is Mrs. Marteen?" he demanded hoarsely.

The servant shook his head. "She left two hours ago, at least," he answered, with a glance toward the hall clock.

"What did she say - what message did she leave?" Gard pushed by him impatiently, making for the stairs leading to the upper floor and the library.

The butler stared. "Why, nothing, sir. She asked for Miss Dorothy, and when none of us could tell her where she went, or why - which we all thought queer enough, sir - she didn't seem surprised; so I suppose she knows, sir. Madam just went upstairs to the library first, and then to Miss Dorothy's room - the maid saw her, sir - and then she came down and went out. She had on a heavy veil, but she looked scarce fit to stand for all that, and she went - never said a word about her baggage or anything - just went out to the cab that was waiting. Then about a half hour later, Mary, her maid, came in with the boxes. I hope there's nothing wrong, sir?"

Gard listened, his heart tightening with apprehension. "Call White Plains, 56," he ordered sharply. "Tell Miss Dorothy to come at once and then send for me, quick, now!" he commanded; and as the wondering flunky turned toward the telephone, he sprang up the stairs, threw open the library door and entered. The electric lights were blazing in the heat and silence of the closed room. The odor of violets hung reminiscent in the stale air. The panel by the mantelpiece was thrust back, and the door of the safe, so uselessly concealed, hung open, revealing the empty shelves within and the deep shadow of the inner compartment. He saw it all in a flash of understanding; the frantic woman's rush to the place of concealment, - the ravaged hiding place. What could she argue, but that all that her enemy had planned had befallen? Her child knew all, and had gone - fled from her and the horror of her life, leaving no sign of forgiveness or pity.

Sick, and faint, Gard turned away. One door in the corridor stood open, left so, he divined, by the hurried passing of the mother from the empty nest, Dorothy's room, all pink and white and girlish in its simplicity. One fragrant pillow, with its dainty embroidered cover, was dented, as if still warm from the burning cheek that had pressed it in an agony of loss. Nothing about the chamber was displaced; only an empty photograph frame lying upon the dressing table told of the trembling, pale hands that had bereft it of its jewel. She had taken her little girl's picture with the heartbroken conviction that never again would she see its original, or that those girlish eyes would look upon her again save in fear and loathing. The empty case dropped from his hands to the silver-crowded, lace-covered table; he was startled to see in the mirror, hung with its frivolous load of cotillion favors and dance cards, his own face convulsed with grief, and turned, appalled, from his own image. His resourceful brain refused its functions. He could not guess her movements after that silent, definitive leave taking. He could but picture her tall, erect figure, outwardly composed and nonchalant, as she must have stood, facing the outer world, looking out to what - to what? A mad hope rose in his breast. Would she turn to him? Would her instinctive steps lead her to seek his protection.

Yes. He must be where she could find him; he must be within reach. It could not be that she would pass thus silently into some unknown life - or - He would not concede the other possibility.

Turning blindly from the room, he descended to the lower floor, where the butler, with difficulty suppressing his curiosity, informed him that Miss Dorothy had answered that she would return to town at once.

Gard hesitated, then turned sharply upon the servant. "Your mistress has been ill, as you know. We have reason to believe that she is not quite herself. If you learn anything of her, notify me at once. No matter what orders she may give, you understand, or no matter how slight the clew - send for me."

Once again in the street, he paused, uncertain. His eye fell upon Denning's limousine drawn up behind his waiting cab. Fury at this espionage sent him toward it. Thrusting his face In at the open window, he glared at his pursuer.

"What are you here for?" he snarled.

Denning looked at him coldly. "To see that you keep faith, that's all. Your personal concerns must wait. Have you forgotten that you are to take the midnight train to Washington? I'm here to see that you do it."

Gard wrenched open the door of the car. "You are, are you? Let the whole damned thing go!" he cried. "Send your proxies. This is a matter of life and death!"

"I know it," said Denning; "it is - to a lot of people who trust you; and you are going to do your duty if I have to kidnap you to do it. You have two hours before your train leaves. My private car is waiting for you. Make what plans you like till then; but I'll not leave you; neither will Langley - he's following you, too. Come, buck up. Are you mad that you desert in the face of shipwreck?"

Gard turned suddenly, ordered his taxi to follow and got in beside Denning. His mood and voice were changed. "I've got to think. Don't speak to me. Get me home as soon as you can."

He leaned back, closed his eyes and concentrated all his energies. In the first place, Denning was right - he must not desert, even with his own disaster close upon him. He owed his public his life, if necessary. As a king must go to the defense of his people in spite of every private grief or necessity, so he must go now. The very form of his decision surprised him. He realized that his yearning for another soul's awakening had awakened his own soul. He had willed her a conscience and developed one himself. But, his decision reached with that sudden precision charac-teristic of him, his anxious fears demanded that every possible precaution be taken, every effort made that could tend to save or relieve the desperate situation he must leave behind him. First of all his physician - to him he must speak the truth, and to him alone. Brencherly should be his active tool. Mahr must be impressed.

Springing from the motor at his own door, he snapped an order to his butler, and sent him with the cab to bring the doctor instantly. Once in the library, he telephoned for the detective. He then called up Victor Mahr, requested that however late he might call, a visitor be admitted at once, on a matter of the first importance and received the assurance that his wishes would be complied with; he asked Denning, who had followed him, to wait in another room, thrust back the papers on his table and settled himself to write.

"No one knows anything," he scrawled, "neither Dorothy nor anyone else." With succinct directness he covered the whole story - explained, elucidated. Through every word the golden thread of his deep devotion glowed steadily. Would the letter ever reach her? Would her eyes ever see the reassuring lines? He refused to believe his efforts useless. She must come. He sealed and directed the letter, as Brencherly was admitted. Gard turned and eyed the young man sharply, wondering how much, how little he dared tell him.

"Brencherly," he said slowly, "I'm giving you the biggest commission of your life. You've got to take my place here, for I'm going to the front. I've got to rely on you, and if you fail me, well, you know me - that's enough. Now, I want discretion first, last and all the time. Then I want foresight, tact, genius - everything in you that can think and plan. Here are the facts: Mrs.

Marteen has come back - suddenly. She's been ill. Her mind, from all I can learn, is affected. She has delusions; she may have suicidal mania. She has disappeared, and she must be found - as secretly as possible. Her delusions and illness must not become a newspaper headline. I needn't tell you it would make 'a story.' There's one chance in fifty that she may come here, or telephone for me. You are not to leave this room. Answer that telephone - you know her voice, don't you? You are to tell her that I have her letter and she has nothing to worry about; that I have had charge of all her affairs in her absence; that her daughter knows of her return and wants her at once. Tell her that I have left a letter for her - this one. When Miss Marteen calls up, tell her to go to her home; that her mother has come back, but has left again, and is ill; that I'm doing all in my power to find her. Tell her to call me at once on the long distance telephone to Washington, at the New Willard. Wherever I have to be I'll arrange that I can be called at once. Do you understand?

"Dr. Balys will be here in a few moments. He will have the hospitals canvassed. If you locate her, Brencherly, send my doctor to her at once. Get her to her own apartment, and don't let her talk. I want you to pick a man to watch the morgue; to look up every case of reported suicide that by any chance might be Mrs. Marteen - here or in other cities." Gard felt the blood leave his heart as he said the words, though there was no quaver in his voice. "If they should find her, don't let her identity be known if there is any chance of concealing it, not until you reach me. Don't let Miss Marteen know. Put another man on the hotel arrivals. She left St. Augustine - Here - " He - jotted down times and dates on a slip. "Work on that. Keep the police off. I'll have Balys stay here, unless he locates her in any of the hospitals. My secretary is yours; and there are half a dozen telephones in the house; you can keep 'em all going. But, mind, there must be no leak. Watch her apartment, too. Question her maid up there. Of course that letter on the table there might interest you, but I think I had better trust you, since I make you my deputy. This is no small matter, Brencherly. Honesty is the best policy - and there *are* rewards and punishments."

The strain of grief and anxiety had set its mark on Gard's face. His deadly earnestness and evident effort at self-control sent a thrill of pitying admiration through the detective's hardened indifference. A rush of loyalty filled his heart; he wanted to help, without thought of reward or punishment. He felt hot shame that his calling had deserved the suspicion his employer cast upon it.

"I'll do my honest best," he said with such dear-eyed sincerity that Gard smiled wanly and held out his hand.

"Thank you," he said simply.

The interview with the doctor lasted another half-hour. Time seemed to fly. Another hour and he must leave to others the quest that his soul demanded. Unquestioning and determined, Denning took him once more in the limousine. They were silent during the drive to Victor Mahr's address. Gard descended before the house, leaving Denning in the car.

"Don't worry," he said as he closed the door of the automobile. "I'll not be long; I give you my word."

Denning smiled. "That's all that's wanted in Washington, old man. You've got a quarter of an hour to spare."

Denning switched on the electric light and, taking a bundle of papers from his inside pocket, began to pencil swift annotation.

Gard ran lightly up the steps. It was quite on the cards that Mrs. Marteen in her anguish and despair might make an effort to see and upbraid the man whose hatred and vengeance had wrecked her life. Mahr must be warned of all that had taken place, and schooled to meet the situation - to confess at once that his plans had been thwarted, that his tongue was forever bound to silence and that his intended victim was free. He, Marcus Gard, must dictate every word that might be said, foresee every possible form in which a meeting might come, and dictate the terms of Mahr's surrender. Words and sentences formed and shifted in his mind as he waited impatiently for his summons to be answered. The butler bowed, murmuring that Mr. Mahr was expecting Mr. Gard, and preceded him across the anteroom to the well-remembered door of the inner sanctum, which he threw open before the guest, and retired silently.

Closing the door securely behind him, Gard turned toward the sole occupant of the room. Mahr did not heed his coming nor rise to greet him. The ticking of the carved Louis XV clock on the mantel seemed preternaturally loud in the oppressive silence.

Suddenly and unreasonably Gard choked with fear. In one bound he crossed the room and stood staring down at the face of his host. For an instant he stood paralyzed with amazement and horror. Then, as always, when in the heart of the tempest, he became calm, and his mind, as if acting under some heroic stimulant, became intensely clarified. Mahr was dead. He leaned forward and lifted the head; the body was still warm, and it fell forward, limp and heavy. On the left temple was a large contusion and a slight cut. The cause was not far to seek. On the table lay an ancient flintlock pistol, somewhat apart from a heap of small arms belonging to an eighteenth century trophy.

Murder! Murder - and Mrs. Marteen! His imagination pictured her beautiful still face suddenly becoming maniacal with fury and pain. Gard suppressed an exclamation. Well, he would swear Mahr was alive at half after eleven, when he had seen him. If anyone knew of her coming before that, she would be cleared. No one knew of his own feud with Mahr; no one suspected it. His word would be accepted.

Mahr's face, repulsive in life, was hideous in death - a mask of selfishness, duplicity and venomous cunning from which departing life had taken its one charm of intelligence. He looked at the wound again. The blow must have been sudden and of great force. Acting on an impulse, he tiptoed to one of the curtained windows, unlocked the fastening and raised it slightly. A robbery - why not? Silently moving back into the room, he approached the corpse and with nervous rapidity looted the dead man of everything of value, leaving the torn wallet, a wornout crumpled affair, lying on the floor. He opened and emptied the table drawers, as if a hurried search had been made. Slipping the compromising jewels into his overcoat pocket, he turned about and faced the room like a stage manager judging of a play's setting. The luxurious furnishings, the long mahogany table warmly reflecting the lights of the heavily shaded lamp; the wide, gaping fireplace; the lurking shadows of the corners; the curtain by the opened window bellying slightly in the draught; above, in the soft radiance of the hooded electrics, the glowing, living, radiant personality of the Vandyke; below, the stark, evil face of the dead, with its blue bruised temple and blood-clotted hair.

Gard strove to reconstruct the crime as the next entrant would judge it - the thief gliding in by the window; the collector busy over the examination of his curios; the blow, probably only intended to stun; the hasty theft and stealthy exit.

His heart pounded in his breast, but it was with outward calm that he crossed the threshold, calling back a "Good-night," whose grim irony was not lost upon him. In the hall, as he put on his hat, he addressed the servant casually:

"Mr. Mahr says you may lock up and go. He does not want to be disturbed, as he has some papers that will keep him late. Remind Mr. Mahr to call me at the New Willard in the morning; I may have some news."

As he left the house he staggered; he felt his knees shaking. With a superhuman effort he steadied himself - Denning must not suspect anything unusual. He descended the steps with a firm tread, and pausing at the last step, twisted as if to reach an uncomfortably settled coat collar - his quick glance taking in the contour of the house and the probability of access by the window. The glimpse was reassuring. By means of the iron railing a man might readily gain the ledge below the first floor windows. He entered the limousine and nodded to Denning.

"All right," he said. "On to Washington."

*   *   *   *   *

XI

Through the long, hours of the night Gard lay awake, living over the gruesome moments spent in the ill-omened house on Washington Square. The ghastly face of the dead man seemed to stare at him from every corner of the luxurious room.

Had he done wisely, Gard wondered, in setting the scene of robbery? Had he done it convincingly? That he could become involved in the case in another character than that of witness, occurred to him, but he dismissed it with a shrug. He was able, he felt, to cope with any situation. Nevertheless, the valuables he had taken from the corpse seemed to take on bulk. He thanked his stars that his valet was not with him - at least he would not have to consider the ever present danger of discovery. He had hoped to dispose of the compromising articles while crossing the ferry, but when, on his suggestion of the benefits of cool night air, he had descended from the motor and advanced to the rail, Denning had accompanied him and remained at his elbow, discussing future moves in their giant financial game. Once on board the private car, he had considered disposing of the jewels from the car window or the observation platform, but abandoned that scheme as worse than useless. The track walkers' inevitable discovery would only bring suspicion upon someone traveling along the line - and who but himself must eventually he suspected?

There was nothing for it but to break up the horde piece by piece and lose the compromising gems in unrecognizable fragments. The impulse was upon him to switch on the electrics and begin the work of destruction here in his stateroom at once. But he feared Denning; he feared Langley. Then his thoughts reverted to Mrs. Marteen. Where was she? Where was she hiding? Had she made away with herself after her desperate deed? His heart ached and yearned toward her while his senses revolted in horror of the crime. His world was torn asunder. The awful discovery he had made had once and for all precluded a change of plans. Sudden resistance on his part would have been enigmatical to Denning - or he must confess the state of affairs in the silent house he had just left. At least by his ruse he had gained time for her, perhaps even protection.

Her letter, her frantic record of pain and misery, was in his pocket. He found it, and feeling that even if he were observed to be absorbed in reading, it could only appear natural in view of his mission, he propped himself with pillows and reread the tear-blistered pages. His spirit rebelled. No, no; the woman who had written those searing, bitter lines of awakening could not be guilty of monstrous murder. He hated himself that his mind had accused her. He cursed himself that by his intervention he had perhaps thrown investigation upon the wrong scent, while the truth, he assured himself, must exonerate her and bring the real criminal to justice. What could have made him be such a fool? The next instant he thanked his stars that he had been cool enough to plan the scene. As he read the throbbing pages, tears rose to his eyes again and again;

he had to lay the letter down and compose himself. Ah, he was wrong, always at fault. By his well-intended interference, he had arranged Dorothy's flight, with results he trembled to foresee. And Dorothy! What was he to tell the child? How was he to prepare her to bear the present strain and the knowledge of what might come?

The fevered hours passed slowly. It was with a wrenching effort that he forced his mind to concentrate on the business in hand for the coming day. Yet, for his own honor and the sake of his people, it must be done, and well done. Moreover, there must be no wavering on his part, nothing to let anyone infer an unusual disturbance of mind. He must be prepared to play shocked surprise when the tragic news reached him.

Utter exhaustion finally overpowered his fevered brain and he fell into a troubled sleep, from which he was aroused by Denning's voice. The car was not in motion, and he divined that it had been shunted to await their pleasure. He dressed hastily, his heart still aching with dread and uncertainty.

As he faced himself in the mirror he noted his sunken eyes and ghastly color, and Denning, entering behind him, noted it, too, with a quick thrill of sympathy. He had come to accept as fact his fear, expressed in the directors' room. Gard must be suffering from some deadly disease.

"You look all in, Gard," he said regretfully. "I'm sorry I had to drive you so." He hesitated. "Has - have the doctors been giving you a scare about yourself?"

Gard divined the other's version of his strange actions,

and jumped at an excuse that explained and covered much.

"Don't talk about it," he said gruffly. "You know it won't do to have rumors about my health going round."

Denning took the remark as a tacit acquiescence. His face expressed genuine sympathy and compassion.

"I'm sorry," he said slowly.

Gard looked up and frowned, yet the kindliness extended, though it was for an imaginary reason, was grateful to him.

"Well, I can take all the extra sympathy anyone has just now," he answered in a tone that carried conviction. "I've had a good deal to struggle against recently - but I'm not whipped yet."

"Oh, you'll be all right," Denning encouraged. "You're a young man still, and you've got the energy of ten young bucks. I'll back you to win. Cheer up; you've got a hard day ahead." Gard nodded. How hard a day his friend little guessed. "We'll go on to the hotel when you are ready. Your first appointment is at nine thirty. Jim is making breakfast for us here."

"All right," said Gard; "I'll join you in a minute. Go ahead and get your coffee." Left alone, he hurriedly pocketed Mahr's jewelry, paused a moment to grind the stone of the scarf pin from its setting - among the cinders of the terminus the gem and its mangled mounting could both be easily lost. His one desire now was to put himself in telephonic communication with New York, but he did not dare to be too pressing.

However, once at the hotel, he made all arrangements to have a call transferred, and opened connection with Brencherly. He was shaking with nervousness. "Any news?" he asked.

"None, Mr. Gard, I'm sorry," the detective's voice sounded over the wire, "except that I've followed your instructions with regard to the young lady. I've not left the 'phone, sir; slept right here in your armchair. The hospitals have been questioned, and there is nothing reported at police headquarters that could possibly interest you. I've looked over the morning papers carefully to see if there was anything the reporters had that might be a clew. There's nothing. I took the liberty of sending Dr. Balys over to the young lady this morning - she seemed in such a state; he'll be back any minute, though. I've got every line pulling on the quiet. I've done my best, sir."

Brencherly's voice ceased, and Gard drew a sigh of relief. At least there was no bad news, and as yet nothing in public print concerning the tragedy. The discovery had probably been made early that morning by the servant, whose duty it was to care for the master's private apartments. The first afternoon papers would contain all the details, and perhaps the ticker would have the news before. He realized that all the haggard night he had been fearing that the morning would bring him knowledge of Mrs. Marteen's death - drowned, asphyxiated, poisoned - the many shapes of the one terrible deed had presented themselves to his subconscious mind, to be thrust away by his stubborn will. Dorothy, summoned to the telephone, had nothing to add to Brencherly's information, but seemed to derive comfort and consolation from Gard's assurances that all would be well. She would call him again at noon, she said.

He came from the booth almost glad. His step was light, his troubled eyes clear once more. He was ready to play his part in every sense, grateful for the respite from his pain. His confidence in himself returned, and he went to the trying and momentous meetings of the morning with his gigantic mental grasp and convincing methods at their best.

Dorothy's message did not reach him till after midday had come and gone. Once Larkin had left the conclave and returned with his face big with consternation and surprise. Gard divined that the news of the murder was out, but nothing was brought up except the business of the corporation.

When at last he left the meeting he motored back to the hotel, refusing the hospitality cordially extended to him, his one desire to be again in touch with events transpiring in New York. He had hardly shown himself in the lobby when a page summoned him to the telephone.

It was Dorothy, her voice faint with fright.

"It's you," she cried - "it's you! Have you learned anything about mother? We haven't any news - nothing at all. Mr. Brencherly and the doctor tell me that everything's being done. But I'm almost wild - and listen; something awful has happened. It's your friend, Mr. Mahr, Teddy's father - he's been murdered!"

"What!" exclaimed Gard, thankful that she could not see his face.

"Yes, yes," she continued, "murdered in his own room - they found him this morning - they say you were the last person to see him before it was done. Oh, Mr. Gard, aren't you coming home soon? It seems as if terrible things happen all the time - and I'm frightened. Please, come back!"

The voice choked in a sob, and her hearer longed to take her in his arms and comfort her, shield her from the terrible possibilities that loomed big on their horizon.

"My darling little girl, I'm coming, just as fast as I can. I wouldn't be here, leaving you to face this anxiety alone, if I could possibly help it - you know that, dear," he pleaded. "I've one more important, unavoidable interview; then my car couples on to the first express. Give Teddy all my sympathy. I can hardly realize what you say. Why, I saw him only last night just before I took the train. Keep up your courage, and don't be frightened."

"I'll try," came the pathetic voice; "I will - but, oh, come soon!"

Gard excused himself to everyone, pleading the necessity of rest, and once alone in his room, set about ripping and smashing the incriminating evidence, until nothing but a few loose stones and crumpled bits of gold remained. He broke the monogrammed case of the watch from its fastening and crushed its face. Now to contrive to scatter the fragments would be a simple matter. He secreted them in an inner pocket, and his pressing desire of their destruction satisfied, he telephoned to Langley to join him in his private room at a hurried luncheon. Next he sent for the afternoon papers. Not a line as yet, however; and Langley and Denning having evidently decided it to be unwise to deflect his thoughts from matters in hand, did not mention Mahr. Even when he brought up the name himself with a casual mention of the possibility of acquiring the Heim Vandyke, there was nothing said to give him an opportunity to speak and he was breathless for details, to learn if his ruse had succeeded. At last he called Brencherly, both Denning and Langley endeavoring to divert him from his intention.

"Yes, yes," snapped Gard; "what's the news?"

His companions exchanged dubious glances.

"Nothing learned yet about the matter, sir, on which you engaged me, nothing at all. But - there's something else - I think you ought to know - Victor Mahr is dead!"

"Dead! How? When?" Gard feigned surprise.

"Murdered last night," came the reply. "Found this morning. Our man watching the house learned it as soon as anyone did. A case of robbery, they say - but the coroner's verdict hasn't been given yet. He was hit in the head with a pistol - but - I think, sir, they'll want you; you saw him last night, they say - after you left me. Have you any instructions to give me, sir?"

Gard reflected. "I don't know," he wavered. "Hold all the good men in your service you can for me - and remember what I told you." He turned to the two men. "Mahr's dead - murdered!" he blurted out, as if startled by the news.

They nodded. "Yes, we knew. But," Denning added, "we didn't want to upset you any further. It came out on the ticker at eleven. How are you feeling?" he asked with friendly solicitude. "I wish you'd eat something - you've not touched anything but coffee for nearly twenty-four hours."

"I can't," said Gard grimly. "Let's go to the Capitol and get it over with. Have you 'phoned Senator Ryan? I'm all right," he assured them, as he caught sight of Langley's dubious expression. "I want to get through here as quickly as possible and get back. I suppose you realize that I'll be wanted in the city in more ways than one. I was the last person, except the murderer, to see Mahr. Come on."

As they came from the Capitol at the close of their conference, Langley and Denning fell behind for a moment.

"What a wonder the man is!" exclaimed Denning with enthusiasm. "Sick as he is, and with all these other troubles on him, he's bucked up and buffaloed this whole thing into shape. He forgets nothing!"

Gard entered the motor first, and, as he leaned forward, dropped from the opposite window a fragment of twisted gold. An hour later, in the waiting room they had traversed, a woman picked up a pigeon blood ruby, but the grinding wheels of trains and engines had left no trace of the trifles they had destroyed. In the yard near the private siding, a coupling hand came upon a twisted gold watch case, so crushed that the diamond monogram it once had boasted was unrecognizable.

"At every stop, Jim," said Gard, as he threw himself

wearily into a lounging chair in the saloon end of the car, "I want you to go out and get me all the latest editions of the New York papers."

The negro bowed, disappeared into the cook's galley and returned with glasses and a bottle of champagne. He poured a glass, which Gard drank gratefully.

Gard heard Langley and Denning moving about their stateroom. The noise of the terminal rang an iron chorus, accompanied by whistles and the hiss of escaping steam. The private car was attached to the express, and the return journey began. His irritated nerves would have set him tramping pantherwise, but sheer weariness kept him in his chair. Presently his fellow travelers joined him, but he took little or no heed of their conversation. Once he drank again, a toast to the successful issue of their combined efforts. He lay back, striving to control his rising anxiety. What would the story be that would greet him from the heavy leads of the newspapers?

"Baltimore - Baltimore - Baltimore" - the wheels seemed to pound the name from the steel rails; the car rocked to it. By the time they reached that city the New York afternoon editions would have been distributed. At last they glided up to the station and the porter swung off into the waiting room. Gard rose and stood waiting, chewing savagely on his unlighted cigar.

"It's Mahr," he apologized to Denning. "I want to learn the facts." His hand shook as he snatched the smudgy sheets from the negro.

In big letters across the front page he caught the headline:

MURDER OF VICTOR MAHR

FAMOUS CLUBMAN AND FINANCIER
STABBED TO DEATH IN HIS OWN LIBRARY

EVIDENCE OF ROBBERY

WOMAN SUSPECTED OF THE CRIME

"Stabbed to death ... Woman suspected." His brain reeled. How "stabbed to death"? He himself had seen - "Woman suspected." Then all his despairing efforts to save her had been in vain! The train, starting suddenly, gave him ample excuse to clutch the back of the chair for support, and to fall heavily upon its cushions. He could not have held himself upright another moment. An absurd scheme flashed through his brain. He would, if necessary, take the blame upon himself - anything to shield her. He would say they had quarreled over the Vandyke.

He became aware that Denning was asking for one of the three papers he was clutching. He gave it to him, suddenly realizing that he was not alone. He knew his face was deathly, and he could feel his heart's slow pound against his ribs. If they did not believe him a sick man, they must believe him a guilty one. To control his agitation seemed impossible. The page swam before his eyes, and it was some moments before he could focus upon the finer print of the sensational article.

The gruesome discovery was made by a servant, entering the library at eight that morning. She found her master lying in the chair and thought him asleep. She knew that the night before he had dismissed the butler, declaring his intention to sit up late over some important business. He might have been overcome by weariness. She tiptoed out and went in search of the valet. His orders had been to call his master at nine and he hesitated about waking him earlier, but at last decided to do so, as it was nearing the hour. On entering the apartment he had noticed the disorder of the room. He put out the electric light from the switch by the door, drew the curtains and raised the blind. At once he realized that death confronted him. Terrified, he had rushed to the hall calling for the servants. Theodore Mahr, Victor Mahr's only son, who was on his way to breakfast, rushed at once upon the scene.

There was a cut and contusion on the temple of the victim, evidently inflicted by a weapon lying upon the table, which was believed to be the cause of death, until the arrival of the coroner and Mr. Mahr's own physician, when it was discovered that the victim's heart had been pierced by a very slender blade or stiletto. The wound was so small and the aperture closed by the head of the weapon in such a manner that no blood had issued.

An enterprising reporter had gained access to the chamber of death, and described in detail the rifling of the drawers, the partially open window; he had picked up a small gold link, evidently torn from the sleeve buttons of the deceased. Mr. Mahr was last seen alive by his friend, Marcus Gard, who called to see him on important business before taking his departure to Washington. Just prior to this, however, a strange woman, heavily veiled, had sent in a note and been admitted to Mr. Mahr. This woman was not seen to leave the house; in fact, the servant had supposed her present when Mr. Gard called, and a party to the business under discussion; it was now believed that she might have remained concealed in the outer room until after the great financier had taken his departure. Of this, however, there was no present evidence. Mahr had dismissed the butler and told him to lock up - yet the woman had not been seen to leave. Of course she could have let herself out, or Mr. Mahr could have opened the door for her - no one seemed to recall whether the chain was on in the morning or not.

Was the crime one of anger or revenge? Why, then, the robbery? The appearance of the table drawers would seem to indicate someone in search of papers, yet the dead man's valuables appeared to have been removed by force - the cuff link had been broken, the watch snatched from its pocket with such violence that the cloth had been torn. At present the mystery that surrounded the crime was impenetrable. The dead man's son was prostrated with grief.

Gard finished reading and rose, crushing the paper in his hand. "It's a horrible thing - horrible! I hope you gentlemen will excuse me. I am not well, and this - has affected me - unaccountably." He turned to his stateroom. "I'm going to rest, if I can."

The two men looked at each other in deep concern.

"I hope we don't lose him," muttered Denning.

Alone in the silence of his swaying room, Gard threw himself face down upon the bed. He could not reason any longer. His whole being gave way to a voiceless cry. He shook as if with cold, and beat his hands rhythmically on the pillows. He rolled over at last, and lay staring at the curved ceiling of the car. One thought obsessed him. She had been there, in that room, hidden - watching him, doubtless, as he committed the ghastly theft. Even in the awful situation in which she found herself, what must she think of *him*? Criminal, blackmailer, murderess, perhaps - but what could she think of him? The blood tingled through his veins and his waxen face flushed scarlet with vivid shame. In his weakened, overwrought condition, this aspect of the case outranked all others. He forgot the horrible publicity that threatened not only Dorothy and her mother but Victor Mahr's son - when the motive of the crime was learned. He forgot the yearning of his soul for the saving of its sister spirit. He forgot the dread vision of the chair of death in the keen personal shame of the creature she must believe him to be.

Suddenly a new angle of the case presented itself - Brencherly! He sat up gasping. Brencherly must have guessed - the inevitable logic of the situation led straight to the solution of the enigma. The detective knew of Mahr's efforts to obtain the combination of Mrs. Marteen's safe; he, himself, had told him that those efforts had been successful. Brencherly knew of Mrs. Marteen's sudden return, her visit to her home and her mysterious disappearance. The motive of the murder was supplied, the disappearance accounted for. Already the detective's trained mind had doubtless pieced together the fragments of these broken lives. It was Brencherly who had told him of Mahr's former marriage. Everything, everything was in his hands. Would the man remain true to him? What wouldn't one of the great newspapers pay for the inside story! Could Brencherly be trusted? His well seasoned dislike of the whole detective and police service made him sure of treachery. But before him rose the vision of the boyish, candid face, as the detective had taken the Great Man's proffered hand, the honesty in his voice as he had given his word - "I'll do my best, sir," and into Gard's black despair crept a pale ray of hope.

Gard had not been mistaken when he surmised that Brencherly must inevitably connect the murder with the sequence of events. But the conclusion reached with relentless finality by that astute young man was far from being what Gard had feared. To the detective's mind the answer was plain - his employer was guilty.

The motive obviously concerned Mrs. Marteen. It was evident, from Mahr's efforts to gain access to that lady's safe, that she possessed something of which Mahr stood in fear or desired to possess. It was possible that she had obtained proof against Mahr. Perhaps she opposed young Teddy's attentions to her daughter. Perhaps Mahr was responsible for the disappearance. At any rate, Gard had been the last person to see Mahr as far as anyone knew; and a bitter feud existed, which no one guessed. Brencherly did not place great reliance in the woman theory. Doubtless one had called, but she had probably left. That she had gone out unseen was no astonishing matter. A servant delinquent in his hall duty was by no means a novelty even in the best regulated mansions. The robbery in that case could have been only a blind for an act of anger or revenge. The search for papers might have a deeper significance.

He intended to "stand by the boss," Brencherly told himself. Gard was a great man and a decent sort; Mahr was an unworthy specimen. Brencherly decided that at all Costs Marcus Gard must be protected. He cursed the promise that kept him at his post. He longed to get into personal touch with every tangible piece of evidence, every clew, noted and unnoted. His men were on the spot and reporting to him; but that could not make up for personal investigation. In view of these new developments, what would be Mrs. Marteen's next move? Some secret bond connected the three - Mahr, Gard and Mrs. Marteen.

Brencherly, alone in Gard's library, rose and paced the room, glancing at the desk clock every time his line of march took him past the table. His employer was coming home fast as steam could bring him. He longed for his arrival and the council of war that must ensue; longed to be relieved of the tedium of room-tied waiting. He no longer looked for any communication from Mrs. Marteen. She had her reasons for conceal-ment, no doubt, and he felt assured that neither hospital nor morgue would yield her up. It was with genuine delight that he at last heard the familiar voice on the telephone, though it was but a hurried inquiry for news.

Half an hour later, haggard and worn beyond belief, Gard hurried into the library and held out his hand.

The young man looked at his face in astonishment as Gard threw himself into the chair and turned toward him.

"You'll pardon me," he faltered. "There's nothing that can't wait, and you need rest, sir."

"Not till I can get it without nightmares," he snapped. "Now give me this Mahr affair - all of it. I've seen the papers, of course, but I imagine you have the inside; then I want to hear what you think."

The detective gave a start and colored to the roots of his hair. No doubt about it, Gard was a great man, if he could meet such a situation in such a manner and get away with it.

"Well, sir, the papers have it straight enough this time, as it happens. There's nothing different."

"What was the weapon?"

"A stiletto paper cutter, that he always had on his table. It had a top like a fencing foil; in fact, that's what it was in miniature, except that it was edged. It was that top, flattened close down, that stopped any flow of blood, so that everyone thought at first it was the blow on the temple that killed him. There's this about it, though: I'm told they say he was stunned first and stabbed afterward. That doesn't look like the work of a common thief, does it?"

His hearer could not control a shudder. "Why not?" he parried. "He may have known the knockout was only temporary, and he was afraid he'd come to; or the man might have been known to Mahr, and he'd recognized him."

Brencherly shook his head incredulously.

"And the woman? What description did the servants give?" There was a perceptible pause before he asked the question.

"The woman? The description is pretty vague - dressed in black, a heavy veil, black gloves; nothing extra-ordinary. The servant did say he thought her hair was gray, or it might have been light. He caught a glimpse of the back of her head when he showed her into the room. She sent in a note first; just a plain envelope; it wasn't directed."

"Did they find any letter or enclosure that might explain why she was admitted?"

"No, sir, nothing."

The two men eyed each other in silence. Each felt the other's reticence.

"And what do you advise now?" Gard inquired.

Brencherly's gaze shifted to the bronze inkwells.

"If I knew just how this event affected you, sir, I might be able to advise."

It was his employer's turn to look away.

"I know absolutely nothing about the cause of Mahr's death. I do know that there was no love lost between us; also that I was the last person known to have been with him. Isn't that enough to show you how I am affected?"

"And the motive of your quarrel?" The detective felt his heart thump and wondered at his own daring.

"We were rival competitors for the Heim Vandyke - he got it away from me."

"Does that answer my question, sir?" Again Brencherly gasped at his own temerity.

"Young man," bellowed Gard, half rising from his chair, "what are you trying to infer?"

Brencherly stood up. "Please, Mr. Gard, be frank with me. I want to help you; I want to see you through. It can be done - I'm sure of it. No one knows about your trouble with Mahr. What he wanted with the combination of that safe I can't guess, but it was for no good; and you told me yourself that he had secured it. But everything may work out all right if you let me help you. I'm used to this cross-examination business, and I can coach you so they won't get a thing. I don't pretend to be in a class with you, sir; don't think I'm so conceited. I'm just specialized, that's all. I want to help, and I can if you'll let me."

Gard's face underwent a kaleidoscopic series of changes; then astonishment and relief finally triumphed, and were followed by hysterical laughter. Brencherly was disconcerted.

"Oh, so you think *I* did it!" he said at last. "I wish I had!" he added. "That wouldn't worry me in the least."

"Mrs. Marteen!" Brencherly exclaimed, and stood aghast and silent.

"No!" thundered Gard, and then leaned forward brokenly with his head in his hand.

Slowly the detective's mind readjusted itself, and the look in his eyes fixed upon Gard's bowed figure was all pitying understanding. Then he shook his head.

"No, she didn't do it," he said - "never! I don't believe it!"

The stricken man looked up gratefully, but his head sank forward again. "He had done a horrible thing to her," he said. "You're right; you must have my confidence if you are to help - us. He had tried to estrange Dorothy from her mother. I - happened to be able to stop that. I used what you told me to quiet him. I threatened to tell his son the whole story. It was bluffing, for we knew nothing positive. But the story is all true. He was putty in my hand when I held that threat over him - putty. I went to him that night to dictate what he was to do in case he obtained any clew of Mrs. Marteen. I thought she might try to see him - to - reproach him. We knew she was very ill, had been when she went away, and then - nerve shock. I went to him - and found him already dead. You understand - Mrs. Marteen - I couldn't but believe - so I set the stage for robbery. I bluffed it off with everyone. I gave the message to lock up and leave Mahr undisturbed. I wanted an alibi for her - or at least to gain time."

Brencherly remained silent. A man's devotion to another commands awed respect, however it may manifest itself. But he was thinking rapidly.

"You know District Attorney Field, don't you?" he asked at length.

Gard nodded. "An old personal friend; but I can't go to him with that story. I'd rather a thousand times he suspected me than give one clew that would lead to her. I'll stick to my story. Field wouldn't cover up a thing like that - he couldn't."

"I know," returned Brencherly; "there's got to be a victim for justice first, or else prove that nothing, not even the ends of justice, can be gained before you can get the wires pulled. But that's what I'm setting out to do. I don't believe, Mr. Gard, that Mrs. Marteen committed that murder - not that there may not have been plenty of reason for it, but the way of it - no! I've got an idea. I don't want to say too much or raise any hopes that I can't make good; but there's just this: when I leave the house it will be to start on another trail. In the meantime, everything is being done that is humanly possible to find Mrs. Marteen. There's only one other way, and that, for the present, won't do - it's newspaper publicity, photographic reproductions and a reward. I think she is somewhere under an assumed name. But there are two lodestones that will draw her if she is able to move. One is the house of Victor Mahr, and the other her own home. There is love and hate to count on, and sooner or later one will draw her within reach. I'll have the closest watch put about that I can devise. There's nothing you can do, sir - now. If you'll rest to-night, you'll be better able to stand to-morrow, and if I can verify my idea in the least I'll tell you. Let your secretary watch here; and good night, Mr. Gard."

*   *   *   *   *

XII

The woman in the narrow bed tossed in a heavy, unnatural sleep. Her lips were swollen and cracked with fever, her cheeks scarlet and dry. She was alone in a narrow, plain room, sparsely but newly furnished. On a dressing table an expensive gold-fitted traveling bag stood open. Over a bent-wood chair hung a costly dark blue traveling suit, and the garments scattered about the room were of the finest make and material. On the floor lay a diamond-encrusted watch, ticking faintly, and a gold mesh bag, evidently flung from under the pillow by the movements of the sleeper. This much the landlady noticed as she softly opened the unlocked door and stood upon the threshold.

"Dear, dear!" she murmured, and, habit strong upon her, she gathered up the scattered garments, folded them neatly, and hung up the gown in the scanty closet, having first examined the tailor's mark on the collar. "Dear, dear!" she said again. "It's noon; now whatever can be the matter? Is she sick? Looks like fever." Again she hesitated and paused to pick up a sheer handkerchief-linen blouse, upon the Irish lace collar of which a circle of pinhead diamonds held a monogram of the same material. "H'm," ruminated the landlady. "Martin! Yes, there's an 'M,' and a 'Y' and a 'J' - h'm! She said she's a friend of Mrs. Bell's, but Mrs. Bell has been in Europe six months. Wonder who her

Ethel Watts Mumford

friends are, if she's going to be sick?"

She moved toward the bed to examine her guest more closely, but her attention was distracted by the luxuriousness of the objects in the dressing case. She fingered them with awe and observed the marking. She stooped for the purse and watch, which she examined with equal attention. Once more her eyes turned to the flushed face on the tumbled pillow. The sleeper had not awakened. The woman leaned over and took one of the restless hands in hers. "It's fever, sure," she said. At the touch and sound of her voice the other opened her eyes, wide with sudden astonishment. "I beg your pardon, Mrs. Martin," said the visitor, "but it's after twelve o'clock, and I began to get anxious - you a stranger and all. I think, ma'am, you've a fever. Better let me call the doctor; there's one on the block."

The woman sat up in bed. "Mrs. Martin?" she said faintly. "Yes - I've - My head hurts - and my eyes - " She stared about her with a puzzled expression that convinced her observer that delirium had set in. "A doctor? Do I need a doctor? Why? What was it the doctor said? That my nerves were in - in - what was it? And I must travel and rest - yes, that was it; I remember now."

"Well," the other woman commented, "he doesn't seem to have done you a world of good, and you better try another."

"No," said Mrs. Marteen with decision, "no, I don't want one - not now, anyway. It's a headache. May I have some tea? Then I'll lie quiet, if you'll lower that blind, please."

"I'm sorry Mrs. Bell's away, or I'd send for her," ventured the landlady.

"Mrs. Bell?" the sick woman echoed with the same tone of puzzled surprise. "Why, she's away - yes - she's away." She sank back among the pillows and waved a dismissing hand.

Still the landlady waited. She deemed it most unwise not to call a doctor, but feared to make herself responsible for the bill if her guest refused. But she had seen enough to convince her that the lady's visible possessions were ample to cover any bill she might run up through illness, provided, of course, it were not contagious. She turned reluctantly and descended to the kitchen to brew the desired tea.

Left alone, the patient sat up and looked about her with strained and frightened eyes. Then she began to wring her hands, slowly, as if such a gesture of torment was foreign to her habit. Her wide, clear brow knitted with puzzled fear. Her lips were distorted as one who would cry out and was held dumb. Presently she spoke.

"Where am I?" There was a long pause of nerve-racking effort as she strove to remember. "*Who* am I?" she cried hysterically. She sprang out of bed and ran to the mirror over the dressing table. The face that looked back at her was familiar, but she could not give it its name. A muffled scream escaped her lips, and she held her clenched fists to her temples as if she feared her brain would burst. "Martin!" she said at last. "Martin - she called me Mrs. Martin. Who is she? When did I come here?"

She seized her dressing case and went through its

Ethel Watts Mumford

contents. Each article was familiar; they were hers; she knew their faults and advantages. The letter case had a spot on the back; she turned it over and found it there. Letter case - the thought was an aspiration. With trembling eagerness she clutched at the papers in the side pocket. Yes, there were letters. She read the address, "Mrs. Martin Marteen" - yes, that was herself. How strange! She had forgotten. The address was a steamer - that seemed possible. There was a journey, a long journey - she vaguely recalled that. But why? Where? She read the notes eagerly; casual *bon voyage* and good wishes; letters referring to books, flowers or bonbons. The signatures were all familiar, but no corresponding image rose in her brain. The last she read gave her a distinct feeling of affection, of admiration, though the signature "M.G." meant nothing. She reread the few scrawled sentences with a longing that frightened her. Who was M.G. - that her bound and gagged mentality cried out for? She felt if she could only reach that mysterious identity all would be well. M.G. would bring everything right.

Suddenly the idea of insanity crossed her mind. She sat down abruptly. The room began to sway; her head ached as if the blows of a hammer were descending on her brow. She clutched the iron foottrail to keep from being tossed from the heaving, rocking bed. The ceiling seemed to lower and crush her. Then an enormous hand and arm entered at the window and turned off the sun which was burning at the end of a gas jet in the room. All was dark.

She recovered consciousness slowly, aware of immeasurable weakness. She lay very still, lying, as it were, within her body. She felt that should she require that weary body to do anything it must refuse. Through her half-closed lids she saw the woman who had first aroused her enter the room with a tray.

"Dear, dear!" she heard her say. "You must cover up. Don't lie on the outside of the bed; get under the covers."

To Mrs. Marteen's intense inner surprise, the weary body obeyed, crawling feebly beneath the sheets. She had not realized that she had lain where she had fainted, at the foot of the bed.

"Now take some tea," the controlling will ordered; "you'll feel better; and a bit of dry toast. Sick headaches are awful, I know, and tea's the best thing."

Once more the body obeyed, and sat up and drank the steaming cup to the great comfort of the inner being. So reviving was its influence that Mrs. Marteen decided to try her own will and speak.

"Thank you - " her lips spoke, and she felt elated. She made another effort. "Thank you very much; it's most refreshing. No - no toast now - but is there some more tea?"

She drank it greedily and lay back upon the pillows with a sigh. Images were forming; memories were coming back now - scraps of things. There was a young girl whom she loved dearly. She had brown hair, very blue eyes and a delicious profile. She was tall and slender. She wore a blue serge suit. Her name - was - was Dorothy. She spread her palms upon the sheet and felt it cool and refreshing.

"I'm afraid I've had a fever," she said slowly. "I think I

Ethel Watts Mumford

have it still. I - I have such nightmares when I sleep - such nightmares." She shuddered.

"Well," said the landlady cheerfully, "you'll feel better now. Take it from me, tea's the thing." She gathered up the napkin, cup and saucer and placed them on the tray. "Well, I'll let you be quiet, and I'll drop in again about five."

Now another memory came, a conscious thought connection. She remembered that Mrs. Bell had told her of her faithful landlady, Mrs. Mellen, with whom she always stopped when she came North; she remembered calling there many times for Mary, her smart motor waking the quiet, unpretentious street. Now she remembered recalling the boarding house and seeking shelter there in her fear and pain. Fear and pain - why, what was it? There was something cataclysmic, overpowering, that had happened. What could it be? Something was hanging over her head, some dreadful punishment. Her struggle to clear the mists from her brain rendered her more wildly feverish, then stupefied her to heavy sleep.

When she awoke again it was to see the kindly fat face of Mrs. Mellen beaming at her from the foot of the bed.

"That's it," she nodded approvingly; "you've had a nice nap. Head's better, I'm sure. Here's another cup of tea, and I brought you up the evening paper; thought you might want to look it over. And if you'll give me your trunk checks, I'll send the expressman after your baggage."

"My trunk checks - what did I do with them? Why, of

course, I gave them to my maid."

A sudden instinct that she did not wish to see her maid, or be followed by her baggage, made her stop short in her speech.

"Oh, your maid!" said Mrs. Mellen. "I'm glad you told me - I'll have to hold a room. You didn't say anything about her last night, so I hadn't made any provision. Dear, dear! And when do you calculate she's liable to get here?"

Mrs. Marteen took refuge in her headache. "I don't know," she said wearily; "perhaps not to-day."

"Oh, well, never mind. I dare say I can manage," Mrs. Mellen assured her. "If you've got everything you want, I'll have to go. Do you think you'll be able to get down to dinner - seven, you know; or would you rather have a plate of nice hot soup up here? Here, I guess. Well, it's no trouble at all, and you're right to starve your head; it's what I always do."

She backed smiling out of the door, which she closed gently.

Mrs. Marteen lay back with closed eyes for a moment, then restlessness seizing her, she sat bolt upright and firmly held her own pulse. "I'm certainly ill," she said aloud. "I wonder where Marie is? Of course I left her at the station, and told her to bring the baggage on. But that was long ago; what has kept her? But this isn't my home," she argued to herself. She was too weak to trouble with further questioning. Instinctively she put out her hand and drew the newspaper toward her. She raised it idly.

Ethel Watts Mumford

"Murder of Victor Mahr" - the big headlines met her eyes.

She felt a shock as if a blinding flash of lightning had enveloped her; she remembered.

She sat as if turned to stone, staring at the ominous words. Her nerves tingled from head to foot; her very life seemed a strained and vibrating string that might snap with any breath. Slowly, as if the Fates had decided not as yet to break that attenuated thread, the tingling, stinging shock passed. She found strength to read the whole article, almost intelligently, though at times her mind would wander to inconsequent things, and the beat of her own heart seemed to deaden her understanding. She remembered now everything, nearly everything, till she turned from her own door, a desperate, homeless outcast. She recalled a cab going somewhere, and then after what appeared to be an interval of unconsciousness, she was walking, walking, instinctively seeking the darkened streets, a satchel in her hand. Somewhere, footsore and exhausted, she had sat upon a bench. Then came the inspiration to go to the quiet house where her friend had stayed. The friend was far away; she could remain there and not be found - stay until she had courage to do the thing that had suggested itself as the only issue - to end it all.

But who had killed Victor Mahr? She gave a gasp of horror and held up her hands - was there blood upon them? But how - how? Try as she would, no answering picture of horror rose from her darkened mind. There was a long, long period she could not account for - not yet; perhaps it would come back, as these other terrible memories had returned to assail her. She rolled over, hiding her face in the pillow, and groaned. The twilight deepened; the shadows thickened in the room.

Suddenly she rose and began dressing in frenzied haste, overcoming her bodily weakness with set purpose. Habit came to her rescue, for she was hardly conscious of her movements. Her toilet completed, she began hastily packing her traveling case, the impulse of flight urging her to trembling speed. But when she lifted the bag its weight discouraged her. Setting it down again upon the dressing table, she lowered her veil and staggered into the dark hallway. Economy dictated delayed illumination in the Mellen household. All was quiet. Somewhat reassured, she descended the stairs, leaning heavily on the rail. The fever which had relaxed for a brief interval renewed its grip, and filled with vague, indescribable fears, she fled blindly. Something in her subconscious brain suggested Victor Mahr, and it was toward Washington Square that she bent her hurried steps.

She entered the park, forcing her failing strength to one supreme effort, and sank, gasping, upon a bench. It faced toward the darkened residence of the murdered man. A few stragglers stood grouped on the pavement before the house, of asked questions of the policeman stationed near by. The electric lights threw lace patterns that wavered over the unfrequented paths. She leaned back, staring at the dark bulk of the mansion with the darker streak at the doorway, which one divined to be the sinister mark of death. Suddenly she sat erect, her aching weariness forgotten. She knew, past peradventure, that *she had sat there upon that very seat the night before*. The memory was but a flash. Already delirium was returning. She was powerless to move. Hours passed, and still she sat staring, unseeing, straight before her. Once a policeman passed and turned to look at her, but her evident refinement quieted his suspicions, and he moved on.

She was roused at last by a movement of the bench as someone took a place beside her. She looked up and vaguely realized that it was a woman, darkly dressed and heavily veiled like herself. She, too, leaned back and seemed lost in contemplation of the house opposite. Presently she raised the veil, as if it obstructed her vision too greatly, revealing a withered face, narrow and long, with a singularly white skin. She had the look of a respectable working woman, and her black-gloved hands were folded over a neat paper package. Her curious glance turned toward the lady beside her, and seemed to find satisfaction in the elegance that even the darkness could not quite conceal. She moved nearer, and with a birdlike twist of the head, leaned forward and frankly gazed in her companion's face. The other did not resent the action.

The woman slowly nodded her head. "Don't know what she's doin', not she. She's one of the silly kind." She put out a hand like a claw, and touched Mrs. Marteen's shoulder. Mrs. Marteen turned her flushed and troubled face toward the woman with something akin to intelligence in her eyes. "What are you settin' here fur, lady?" asked the woman harshly. "Watchin' his house? Well, it's no use; he won't come out again for you or your likes - never again, never again," and she chuckled.

"I was here last night. I sat here last night," said Mrs. Marteen, her mind reverting to its last conscious moment.

The woman peered at her closely , striving to see

through the meshes of the veil where the electric light touched her cheek.

"You did? What fur? Was he comin' out to ye, or did ye want to be let inside?"

The insult was lost on the sufferer.

The woman shifted her position, and changed her tone to one of cunning ingratiation.

"Goin' to the funeral?" she inquired, and without waiting for an answer, continued to talk. "I am. I won't be asked, of course - they don't know I'm here; but I'm goin'. I wouldn't miss it - no, not for - nothing. I ought to have some crape, I know, but I don't see's I can. It would be the right thing, though. I'll ride in a carriage," she boasted. "I suppose they'll have black horses. I haven't seen anything back where I come from, so's I'd know just what *is* the fashionable thing. It'll be a fashionable funeral, won't it? He's a great big man, he is. Everybody knows him - and everybody *don't* know him; but I do - he's a devil I And women love him, always did love him, the fools! Why, *I* used to love him. You wouldn't think that now, would you? Well, I did." She laughed a broken cackle, and seemed surprised that her listener remained mute. "Did you love him?" demanded the crone sneeringly.

"Love him - love him?" exclaimed Mrs. Marteen, her emotions responding where her mind was unreceptive. "I hated him - I hated him!"

"Of course you hated him. How could a lady help hating him?" murmured the questioner. "But would *you* have the courage to kill him - that's what I want

Ethel Watts Mumford

to know!"

Under the inquisition Mrs. Marteen half roused to consciousness. She was in the semi-lucid state of a sleepwalker.

"Kill him!" She held up her hands and looked at them as she had done after reading the account of the murder. "I'm not sure I didn't kill him; perhaps I did - I can't remember - I can't remember," she moaned more and more faintly.

"Don't you take the credit of *that*!" shouted the woman, so loudly that a young man who had been aimlessly walking up and down as if intent upon some rendezvous, stopped short to gaze at them keenly.

The older woman, with a movement so rapid that it seemed almost prestidigitation, lifted and threw back her companion's veil. The young man gave a start and approached hastily, amazement in every feature. But the two women were unaware of his presence, and what he next heard made him pause, turn, and by a slight detour come up close behind the bench.

"Keep your hands off. Don't you say you killed him. What right have *you* to take his life, I'd like to know! Don't let me hear you say that again - don't you dare! Just remember that killing him is *my* business. You sha'n't try to rob me - it's my right!" She leaned forward threateningly.

A hand closed over her wrist. The woman screamed.

"Hold on, Mother, none of that." The young man, still retaining his hold, came from behind the seat and stood over her.

She began to whimper and tremble. "Don't hit me," she begged pitifully. "Don't hit me, and I'll be good, indeed, I will."

Mrs. Marteen had taken no notice of her providential protector. Her head was sunk upon her breast and her hands hung limp in her lap.

The young man whistled twice, never relaxing his hold. A moment later a form detached itself from the group before the door of the house opposite, crossed the street and joined them quickly, yet with no impression of hurry.

"What's up?" the newcomer asked quietly.

"Here, take hold. Don't let her get away from you." With a glance round, he took a hypodermic needle from hi" pocket, and a quick prick in the wrist instantly quieted the struggling, captive. "Get a cab," he ordered, "and bring her over to my rooms. The utmost importance - not a sound to anybody. I've got my job cut out for me - no police in this, mind."

He turned, his manner all gentleness. "Mrs. Marteen - Mrs. Marteen," he repeated. She raised her head slightly. "Will you come with me? My name is Brencherly, and Mr. Gard sent me for you. Come."

She rose obediently. The name he had spoken seemed to inspire confidence, trust and peace, like a word of power; but her limbs refused to move, and she sank back again. Brencherly took her unresisting hand in his, felt her pulse and shook his head.

Ethel Watts Mumford

"Long!" he called. "Get a cab. I'll take Mrs. Marteen; stop somewhere and send a taxi back for you; it might look queer to see two of us with unconscious patients."

When his subordinate turned to go, Brencherly leaned toward the drugged woman, took the bundle from her listless hands and rapidly examined its contents. A coarse nightdress, a black waist and a worn and ragged empty wallet rewarded his search. He tied them up again, put the package in its place and turned once more to Mrs. Marteen. "She's a mighty sick woman," he murmured. "Well, it's home for hers, and then me for the old man."

A taxi drove up, and his assistant descended. With his help Brencherly half supported, half carried his charge to the curb.

Directing the chauffeur to stop at a nearby hotel before proceeding to Mrs. Marteen's apartment, he climbed in beside the patient, and as the machine gathered headway, murmured a fervent "Thank God!"

Mrs. Marteen lay back upon the cushioned seat inert and passive. In the flash of each passing street-light her face showed waxen pale, a cameo against the dark background; so drawn and pinched were her features, that Brencherly, in panic, seized her pulse, in order to assure himself that life had not already fled. Obedient to his orders the cab ran up to an hotel entrance, and Brencherly, leaning out, called the starter.

"Here!" he snapped, "send a taxi over to the park - the bench opposite No. - , and pick up a man with an old lady. She's unconscious."

For an instant the light glinted on his metal badge as he threw back his coat. The starter nodded. Brencherly settled back again in his place with a sigh of relief. It was only a matter of moments now, and he would have brought to an unexpectedly successful close the task he had set himself. He began to build air castles; to construct for himself a little niche in his own selected temple of Fame. He was aroused from his revery by a voice at his side. Mrs. Marteen was speaking, at first indistinctly, then with insistent repetition.

"I can't remember - I can't remember."

He turned to her with gentle questioning, but she did not heed him. Slowly, with infinite effort, as if her slender hands were weighted down, she lifted them before her face. She stared at them with growing horror depicted on her face. He was suddenly reminded of an electrifying performance of Macbeth he had once witnessed. A red glare from a ruby lamp at a fire-street corner splashed her frail fingers with vivid color as they passed it by. She gave a scream that ended in a moan, and mechanically wiped her hands back and forth, back and forth, upon her coat. Brencherly's heart ached for her. Over and over he repeated reassuring words in her deafened ears, striving to lay the awful ghost that had fastened like a vampire on her heart. But to no avail. She was as beyond his reach as if she were a creature of another planet. Never in his active, efficient life had he felt so helpless. It was with thanksgiving that at last he saw the ornate entrance of Mrs. Marteen's home.

"Watch her!" he ordered the chauffeur, as he leaped up the steps and into the vestibule to prepare for her reception.

Ethel Watts Mumford

A message to her apartment brought the maid and butler in haste. With many exclamations of alarm and sympathy they bore her to her own room once more, and laid her upon the bed. She lay limp and still, while they hurried about her with restoratives.

Brencherly was at the telephone. Almost at once, in answer to his ring, Doctor Balys' voice sounded over the wire in hasty congratulations and promises of immediate assistance. Hanging up the receiver, he turned again to his patient.

Through the silent apartment the sound of the doorbell buzzed with sudden shock. The butler stood as if transfixed.

"It's Miss Dorothy!" he exclaimed in consternation. "She went out to walk a little, with young Mr. Mahr. She was nervous and couldn't rest, and telephoned for him to come - in spite of - in spite of - " He hesitated. "Anyway, Mr. Mahr - young Mr. Mahr - came for her, sir. Mr. - Mr. - I think you'd better break it to her, sir. She mustn't see her mother like this - without warning!"

Brencherly ran down the hall, the servant preceding him. As the door swung wide, Dorothy, followed by Teddy Mahr, entered the hallway. She stopped suddenly, face to face with a stranger.

"Who are you? What do you want?" she asked, sudden fear and suspicion in her eyes.

Brencherly explained quickly.

" Mr. Gard employed me, Miss Marteen, to find your

mother, if possible - and - she is here. Don't be alarmed."

Dorothy sank into a chair, weak with relief. Teddy put forth his hand to help her. Instinctively she remained clasping his arm as if his presence gave her strength.

"And she's all right - she isn't hurt - or - or anything?" she implored breathlessly.

"She's very ill, I'm afraid," said Brencherly. "I think you - had better not go to her till the doctor comes. I've sent for him."

"Oh! but I must - I must!" she cried, tears in her voice.

In the rush of happenings no one had thought of Mrs. Mellows. Hers was not a personality to commend itself in moments of stress. Now she suddenly appeared, her eyes swollen with sleep, her ample form swathed in a dressing gown.

"What *is* the matter?" she complained. "I told you, Dorothy, that I thought it very bad form, indeed, for you and Mr. Mahr to go out. In bereavements, such as yours, sir, it's not the proper thing for you to be making exhibitions of yourself. Like as not the reporters have been taking pictures. And at any time they may find out that my poor dear sister is ill and wandering. I don't know *what* to say! The papers will be full of it. And you!" she exclaimed, having for the first time become aware of the detective's presence. "Who are you. How did you get in? I hope and pray you're not a reporter! - Dorothy, don't tell me you've brought a reporter in here - or I shall leave this house at once!"

"No, Aunt, no!" cried Dorothy. "This - this gentleman, has brought my mother home. She's in her room now - she's - "

Mrs. Mellows turned and made a rush down the corridor. Four pairs of hands stayed her in her flight.

"No - no!" begged Dorothy. "This gentleman says she is very ill. We mustn't disturb her - Aunt - please - the doctor is coming."

As if the name had conjured him, a ring announced Doctor Balys' arrival. He entered hastily, his emergency bag in his hand.

"Mr. Brencherly, come with me, please," he ordered. "You can tell me the details as I work. Miss Marteen and Mrs. Mellows, wait for me, and I'll come and tell you the facts just as soon as I know them myself." He nodded unceremoniously and followed Brencherly.

As they neared Mrs. Marteen's room the silence was suddenly broken by a cry. Balys strode past his guide and threw open the door.

Mrs. Marteen, sitting erect in the bed, held out rigid arms as if in desperate appeal. The terrified maid stood by, wringing her hands.

"Gard!" she called. "Marcus Gard! help me! Tell me - I'll believe you - I'll believe you - will you tell me the truth!" Her strength left her suddenly, and as the physician placed a supporting arm about her, she sank back, her eyes closed wearily. As he laid her gently back upon the pillows, she sighed softly, her heavy lids unclosed a moment. "I knew you'd come," she murmured. " You'll take care of - of Dorothy - you will - " Her voice trailed off into nothingness; then "Marcus" - she whispered.

The two men turned away. Brencherly coughed. "Is there any hope?" he asked, breaking the tense silence that seemed suddenly to have entered the room like an actual presence.

The doctor nodded without speaking. "Yes - hope," he said at length, as he opened his leather satchel.

*   *   *   *   *

Ethel Watts Mumford

XIII

It was well into the small hours of the morning when Brencherly sought his own rooms in an inconspicuous apartment hotel, where he, his activities and, at times, strange companions, were not only tolerated, but welcomed. He was weary, but too excited and elated to desire sleep. He nodded to the friendly night clerk, and received a favorable response to his request, even at that unwholesome hour, for coffee and scrambled eggs to be served in his rooms.

He found Long, his assistant, slumbering sonorously in an armchair in the living-room of his modest suite. The open door to the chamber beyond, sufficiently indicated where his charge had been placed.

Long awoke, and stretched himself with a yawn.

"Three o'clock," he observed, with a glance at the mantel clock. "Made a good haul, hey? Well, your kidnapped beauty is in there, dead to the world. I tied her feet together before I went to sleep. You can't tell when they're going to come to, you know, and I thought it would be safer. Now, tell a feller, what's the dope?"

Brencherly entered the adjoining apartment without deigning an answer, switched on the lights and approached the bed. The wizen little woman, with her disheveled white hair and tumbled garments looked pitifully weak and helpless; her thin, claw-like hands clutching at the pillow in a childish pose. Her captor stared at her intently, his brain crowded with strange thoughts. Who was she? What was her history? He had his suspicions, but they all remained to be verified.

He took one of the emaciated wrists in his hand. How frail and small it was, and yet, perhaps, an instrument in the hands of Fate. She moved uneasily, and, glancing down, he noticed how securely she was bound. Leaning over, he loosened the curtain cord with which she had been secured. She sighed as if relieved, and, turning, he left her, as a discreet tapping at his door announced the coming of the meal he had ordered.

A night watchman in shirt sleeves brought in the tray softly and set it upon the table, with a glance of curiosity at the adjoining room. There was usually an interesting story to be gleaned from the guests that the detective brought.

"Come on," said the host eagerly, "fall on it, I'm starved."

"Anything I can do?" inquired the night watchman hopefully.

But Brencherly was still uncommunicative. "Nope, thanks."

"Sure?"

" Yes. Good-night - or good-morning. Tell 'em down

Ethel Watts Mumford

stairs I'm much obliged, as usual."

The two men ate heartily and in silence. It was not till the plates were scraped that either spoke. With the last sip of the soothing beverage Brencherly closed his eyes peacefully.

"Old man," he said, "this night's work is the best luck I've ever had. Now, tell me, did the lady say anything at any time? or did she remain as she is?"

"She didn't say much. Grumbled a little at being moved around; in fact, I thought she was coming out of it for a minute when we first got her in here. Then she straightened out for another lap of sleep. Here's her kit."

He rose as he spoke, and took from the mantel the package she had clung to during all her enforced journey. He untied the parcel, and both men bent over its meager contents. Though Brencherly had seen them under the wavering arc lights of Washington Square, he now gave each article the closest scrutiny. Nothing offered any clew, except the wallet. That, worn as it was, showed its costly texture, and the marks of careful mountings. It was unmistakably a man's wallet, and its flexibility denoted constant use. Brencherly set it on one side.

"Anything else?" he asked.

The other nodded. He had the most important find in reserve.

"These," he said, and drew from his pocket a bunch of newspaper clippings. He laid each one on the table.

"Now, *what* do you think of *that*?" His lean, cadaverous face took on a look of satisfied cunning. If his colleague had not chosen to take him into his confidence, he could show him that he was quite capable of drawing his own inferences and making his own conclusions. He sat back and nonchalantly lit a cigarette.

There were at least twenty cuttings, of all sizes, from a half page from a Sunday supplement to a couple of lines from a financial column. But all bore the name of Victor Mahr more or less conspicuously displayed. Two scraps showed conclusively that they had been cherished and handled more than all the others. One was a sketch of the millionaire's country estate; the other, a reproduction from a photograph of his old-fashioned and imposing city residence.

"H'm!" said Brencherly. "It's pretty clear that she had a reason for occupying that park bench, hey? And she certainly has patronized the news bureau, or been a patient collector herself. See that?" He pushed forward the largest of the clippings. "That's three years old. I remember when that came out. It was after Teddy's sensational playing at the Yale-Harvard game. They had the limelight well turned on then, you remember. And that" - he smoothed another slip - "that announcement of his purchase of 'Allanbrae' is at least five years old. She's been treasuring all this for a long time. Where did you find them?"

"When I put her on the bed," Long replied, "her collar seemed to be choking her, so I loosened it, and a button or two. There was a pink string around her throat and a little old chamois bag - like you might put a turnip-watch in. I took it in here and found - that stuff - what do you think?"

"I think that we're getting near the answer to something we all want to know," said Brencherly. "But it means a lot to a lot of people to keep the police off - for the present. I want to be sure."

"How do you suppose she got in?" said Long, insinuatingly.

"Don't know yet - but we'll find that out. Meantime, don't use the telephone for anything you have to say to anybody. And the other woman, let me tell you, has nothing to do with this case. I'll tell you now, before your curiosity makes you make a fool of yourself - she's been hunted for high and low, because she's had aphasia - forgets who she is, and all that, every once in a while, and her people have been offering a reward. Just happened to make a double haul, that's all. But you don't get in on the first one. Now are you satisfied?" Brencherly looked at his companion quizzically.

Long grunted. He was rather annoyed at having the occurrence so simply explained.

"Oh, well," he yawned, "you're on this case, and I'm only your lobbygow; so I suppose I've got to let it go at that. But, say, I'm tired. Let's turn in, or, if you don't want me in your joint, I'll go down stairs and get them to bunk me somewhere in the dump." He rose. "I suppose they'll fix me up?"

Brencherly went to the telephone and spoke for a moment. "All right," he said; "they'll give you number seventy-three on this floor. I want you to do something for me to-morrow, so set the bellboy for eight o'clock, will you?" A moment later he turned his assistant over to the hotel roundsman, and turned to his own well earned rest. Making a neat packet of the clippings, he stowed them away once more in their worn receptacle - he hesitated, then nodded to himself, having decided to replace them. He must gain this woman's confidence. She must not be made suspicious. Above all, her anger must not be roused. She might become stubborn and uncommunicative. He stepped into the adjoining room and turned on the electrics. The quick flash of the light made him shut his eyes. When he opened them he gave a cry of dismay. The tumbled bed was empty - the window stood wide open. It flashed into his mind, that as he had talked with Long over the incriminating bits of paper, he had felt a draft of air; but his knowledge that his captive was securely tied had eliminated from his mind any idea of the possibility of an attempt at escape. Then, cursing himself, he recalled how he had loosened the cords about her ankles. With a bound he was at the window, looking down at the spidery threads of fire escape ladders, leading down to the utter dark of the service alley.

"My God!" he exclaimed aloud. "My God!" He feared to find a crushed and broken little body at the foot of those steep iron ladders. It seemed impossible for such a frail and aged woman to have, unaided, made her way down the sides of that inky precipice. "Good Lord!" he exclaimed again, "if only she isn't killed!" He stood looking out, leaning as far over the iron railing as he dared, waiting till his eyes should become accustomed to the darkness. Gradually the details of the structure became clear to his vision. No ominous dark mass took shape on the pavement, far beneath. He could vaguely make out the contours of an ash can or two and an abandoned wheelbarrow. But the alley from end to end held no human form. She had succeeded in making her escape! Then at all costs he must find her; and the police must not get hold of her. The evidence of the clippings, her angry words as she prepared to attack Mrs. Marteen - all outlined a possible solution to the tragedy in Washington Square.

He hesitated a moment. His first impulse was to descend the fire escapes in turn and look below for further trace of her going. But he realized that he could reach the alley quicker by going through the house. He cursed himself for a careless fool. How could he have allowed this to happen!

He turned quickly, intent on losing no further moments, when he was frozen into immobility by a sound, the most curiously unexpected of all sounds - a laugh, a faint treble chuckle! It seemed to come from the outer air, from nowhere, to hang suspended in the damp air of the shaft. It was eerie, ghostly. Was the spirit of the dead man laughing at his folly? The detective stepped back on the grating, flattening himself against the outer sill of his window. Again the chuckler - now an unmistakable laugh floated to his ears. With a smothered exclamation he stepped forward again, and looked upward. There, against the violet-gray of the star-sprinkled sky, bulked a crouching shape, cuddled on the landing above.

Brencherly held his breath. It seemed that the woman must fall from her perch, so insecure it seemed. He controlled himself, thinking rapidly. Then he laughed in return.

" That *was* a good joke you played on me," he said.

"How did you ever think of it?"

"Oh," came the answer, punctuated by smothered peals of laughter. "That's the way I got away from the Sanatorium. I just went up instead of down, and stayed there, till they'd hunted all the place over. Then when I saw where they weren't, I just went down and walked out."

"That was clever," he exclaimed. "But you can't be comfortable up there. Won't you come down, and I'll get something for you to eat. You must be hungry, and cold, too."

"No," came the response. "I sort of like it here. It reminds me of the way I fooled them all back there; and they thinking themselves that sharp, too. It's sort of nice, too, looking at the stars - sort of feels like a bird in a nest, don't it?"

"I hope to goodness, she don't take it into her head she can fly," thought Brencherly. Aloud he said: "Say, do you mind if I come up there and sit with you a while? I'm sort of lonesome here myself." He had already moved silently forward, and was slowly mounting the iron ladder - very slowly, a rung at a time, talking all the while in a cordial, friendly voice. He feared she might take fright and precipitate herself to the stones below. But her mood was otherwise.

"I don't mind," she said. "I don't seem to know just how I got here, and perhaps you can tell me. I just woke up and found myself sleepin' on somebody's bed. I thought at first that I was back in the ward, when I found my feet was tied up. Then when I got loose and had time to feel around, I saw 'twas some strange

Ethel Watts Mumford

place. Then the fire escapes sort of looked nice and cool, so I came out."

By this time her visitor had climbed beside her and had seated himself on the landing in such fashion that no move of hers could dislodge either of the strange couple. He noted with relief that they were outside of a door instead of a window, as was the case on all the floors below. The drying roof of the hotel only was above them. He did not wish this extraordinary interview to be interrupted. His airy nest-mate seemed amenable to conversation.

" Well, well!" he resumed, "so *that* was the way you worked it. Wouldn't that make the doctor mad, though - what was the old duffer's name, anyway? You did tell me, but I've got such a poor memory - now, yours is good, I'll bet a hat."

"Well," she said, "'tain't what it used to be, but I'll never forget old Malbey's name as long as I live, nor what he looks like, either. He looks like a potato with sprouts for eyes."

Brencherly laughed. He had a very clear, if unflattering, picture of the learned physician.

"But, say," she cried suddenly, "you're not trying to get me, are you?"

"Oh, *I'm* no friend of the doctor's," he said easily. "Why, I brought you up here to hide you away safely. That was one of my rooms you woke up in. You see, I found you on a bench in the park out there, and you went to sleep so suddenly right while I was talking to you, that I thought you must be tired out."

She leaned forward, peering at him through the dusk. Her white pinched face looked skull-like in the faint light.

"Yes," she said slowly, "seems to me that I remember some woman saying she killed Victor Mahr, and me getting angry about it - and then I don't seem to know just *what* happened. Well, young man, I'm much obliged to you, I'm sure. 'Tain't often an old woman like me gets so well taken care of."

"But why," he questioned softly, "were you so annoyed with the other lady? She had just as much right as you had, I suppose, to kill the gentleman?"

"She had not!" she shrilled. "She had not!" Then lowering her voice to a whisper, she murmured confidentially: "*My* name ain't Welles!"

"Why, Mrs. Welles," he exclaimed, "how can you say so? If you aren't Mrs. Welles, who are you?"

"Just as if you didn't know!" she retorted scornfully.

"Well, perhaps," he admitted. "But never mind that now. Do you know that you lost your bag of clippings?"

Her hand flew to her breast. "Now, gracious me! How could I?"

"Oh, don't worry about them," he soothed. "I've got them all in my room. You shall have them again. Don't you want to come down and get them?" He was cramped and chilled to the bone; moreover, the stars had paled, and a misty fog of floating, impalpable crystal was slowly crossing the oblong of sky left visible by the edifices on both sides of the alley. He waited anxiously for her to reply, but she seemed lost in thought. He looked at her closely. She was asleep, her head resting against the blistered paneling of the door. He shifted his position slightly, and gazed at the coming of the dawn. Gradually the crystal white gave place to faintest violet, then flushed to rose color. The details of the coping above them became sharply distinct. Below them the canyon was full of blue shadow, but already the depths were becoming translucent. He looked at his strange companion. Should he wake her, he wondered. Softly he tried the door. It was locked from within. If he allowed her to slumber in peace, she might, on awakening, be terrified at the visible depths below. Now, all was vague in the blue canyon.

Very gently he pressed her hand and called her. "Mrs. Welles."

She awoke with such a violent start that for an agonized instant he felt his hold slipping. He held her firmly, however, and steadied her with voice and hand.

"Let's go indoors," he said quite casually. "You see if we sit here much longer, it's growing light, and people will see us. Then it won't be easy for me to keep you hidden. Now, if you'll just turn about and let me go first, I'll get you down quite easily and nobody the wiser for our outing."

She looked at him for a moment as if puzzled, then her brow cleared. "Very well, young man," she said. "I must have had a nap. Now, how do you want me to turn?"

He showed her, and with his arms on the outside of the ladder, her body next the rungs - as he had often seen the firemen make their rescues, he slowly steadied her to the landing below and assisted her in at the window.

With a sigh of relief he closed the window behind them and drew down the blinds.

"Now! that's all right, Mrs. Mahr. You're quite safe."

She turned on him her beady eyes and laughed her shrill chuckle. "There, didn't I tell you, you knew all the time? I guess you'll own up that it's the wife who's got the right to kill a husband, won't you?"

"Sure," he said. "I'll see that nobody else gets the credit, believe me!"

*   *   *   *   *

XIV

With Dorothy clinging to his hand, Marcus Gard watched the door of Mrs. Marteen's library with an ever-growing anxiety. Only the presence of the child, who clasped his hand in such fear and grief, kept him from giving way. The long reign of terror that had dragged his heart and mind to the very edge of martyrdom had worn thin his already exhausted nerves, and now - now that the lost was found again, it was to learn by what a slender thread of life they held her with them.

Every moment he could spare from the demands of his responsibilities was spent in close companionship with Dorothy in the house where only the sound of soft-footed nurses, the clink of a spoon in a medicine glass or the tread of the doctor mounting the stairs broke the waiting silence. For many days she had not known them. Now came intervals of consciousness and coherence, but weakness so great that the two anxious watchers, unused to illness, were appalled by the change it wrought. Now for the twentieth time they sat longing for and yet fearing the moment when Dr. Balys, with his friendly eyes and grim mouth, would enter to them with the tale of his last visit and his hopes or fears for the next.

The lamps were lighted, the shades drawn; the fire

crackled quietly on the hearth. The room was filled with the familiar perfume of violets, for Dorothy, true to her mother's custom, kept every vase filled with them.

Silently Gard patted the little cold hand in his, as the sound of approaching footsteps warned them of the doctor's coming. In silence they saw the door open, and welcomed with a throb of relief the smile on the physician's face.

"A great, a very great improvement," he said quickly, in answer to Dorothy's supplicating eyes. "Quite wonderful. She is a woman of such extraordinary character that, once conscious, we can count on her own great will to save the day for us - and to-morrow you shall both see her. To-night, little girl, you may go in and kiss her, very quietly - not a word, you know. Just a kiss and go."

"Now?" whispered Dorothy, as if she were already in the sick room. "May I go now?"

"Yes. No tears, you know, and no huggings - just one little kiss - and then come back here."

Dorothy flew from the room, light and soundless as blown thistledown. The doctor turned to his friend.

"There is something troubling her," he said gravely, "something that is eating at her heart. Ordinarily I wouldn't consent to anyone seeing her so soon; but she called for you in her delirium; and now that she is conscious, she whispers that she must consult you. Perhaps you can relieve her trouble, whatever it is. I'm going to chance it; after Dorothy has seen her, you

Ethel Watts Mumford

may. I don't know exactly what to say, but - well, answer the question in her eyes, if you can - but only a moment - only give her relief. She must have no excitement."

Gard nodded.

"I think I know," he said slowly.

The doctor nodded in understanding, as the girl appeared, her face drawn by emotion.

"Oh, poor mother!" she gasped. "She seemed - so - I don't know why - grateful - to me - thanked me for coming to her - *thanked* me, Dr. Balys, as if I wasn't longing every minute to be with her! She is not quite over her delirium yet, do you think?"

Balys smiled. "Of course she is grateful to see you. Your mother has been very close to the Great Divide, and she, more than any of us, realizes it. Now," he said, turning to Gard, "go in and make your little speech; and, mind you, say your word and go. No conversation with my patient."

Gard stood up, excitement gripping him. He was to see her eyes again, open and understanding. He was to hear her voice in coherent tones once more! The realization of this wonder thrilled him. He went to her presence as some saint of old went to the altar, where, in a dream, the vision of miracle had been promised him. All the pain and torture of the past seemed nothing in the light of this one thing - that she was herself again, to meet him hand to hand and eye to eye. He entered the quiet room and crossed its dimly lighted spaciousness to the bed. The nurse rose tactfully and busied herself among the bottles on the distant dresser.

At last, after the ordeal that they had gone through, in the lonely, hollow torture chamber of the heart, they met, and knew. With a sigh of understanding, she moved her waxen fingers, and, comprehending her gesture, he took her hand and held it, striving to impart to her weakness something of his own vigor. For a moment they remained thus. Then into her eyes, where at first great repose had shone, there came a gleam of questioning. He leaned close above her to catch her whispered words.

"She doesn't know?"

"No," he answered. "Dorothy came to me with his letter. I got everything from the safe, and I sent her away so no further messages might reach her. Now do you see?"

She looked up at him.

Again he took her hand in his and strove to give it life, as a transfusion of blood is given through the veins.

There was silence for a moment. Then her white lips framed a request.

"Bring them - all the things from the inner safe - bring them to-morrow to me." Her eyes turned toward the fire that glowed on the hearth.

He comprehended her intention.

"To-morrow," he murmured, and, turning, softly left the room. With a few words to Dorothy he hurried from the house.

Instinctively he turned to seek the sanctuary of his library, but paused ere he gave the order to his chauffeur. No, before he could call the day complete, there was something else to do. He gave the address of the house on Washington Square. The mansion, as the limousine drew up before it, looked dark, almost deserted. He mounted the steps slowly, his mind crowded with memories - with what burning hatred in his heart he had come to face the owner of that house, to disarm Victor Mahr of his revengeful power. With what primeval elation he had stood upon that topmost step and drawn long breaths of satisfaction at the thought of the encounter in which, with his own hands he had laid his enemy low! Its thrill came to him anew. Again he recalled the hurried purposeful visit that had ended with his finding the enemy passed forever beyond his reach. Vividly he saw before him the silent room - soft lighted, remotely quiet; the waxen hand of a man contrasting with the scarlet damask of a huge winged chair, that hid the face of its owner. And more distinct than all else, staring from the surrounding darkness of the walls, the glorious, palpitating semblance of a warrior of long ago. The strangely living lips, the dusky hollows where thoughtful eyes gleamed darkling. The glint of armor half covered by velvet and fur. A gloved hand that seemed to caress a sword hilt, that caught one crashing ruby light upon its pommel - the matchless Heim Vandyke - the silent, attentive watcher who had seen his sacking of the dead; who seemed, with those deep eyes of under-standing, to realize and know it all - the futile clash of human wills, the little day of love and hate, the infinite mercy, and the inexorable law.

Gard paused, his hand upon the bell. Now at last he could enter this house, and wish it peace. His errand, even the all-comprehending eyes of the dead and gone warrior could look upon without their half-cynic sadness.

As he entered the great silent hall, where the footfalls of the servant were hushed, as if overawed by tragedy, he seemed to leave behind him, as distinctly as he discarded the garment he gave into the lackey's hands, the bitterness of the past. He was ushered into a small and elaborate waiting room to the right. And a moment later Teddy Mahr entered to him, with extended hands.

The boy had aged. His face was white and drawn, but the eyes that looked into Gard's face were courageous and clear.

"Thank you for coming," he said frankly. "Shall we sit here, or - in Father's room?" His mouth twitched slightly. "It really must be part of the house, you know. It was his workshop - and I want it to be mine in the future. I haven't been in there since, and, somehow, if you don't mind, sir, I'd like you to come with me - to be with me, when I first go back."

Gard nodded and smiled rather grimly. "Yes, boy - I'd like to myself. I would have asked it of you, but I feared to awaken memories that were too painful for you. Let us go in. What I have to talk over with you concerns him, too."

They crossed the hall, and Teddy unlocked the heavy door and paused to find the switch. The anteroom sprung into light. In silence they crossed the intervening space to the inner door, which was in turn unlocked.

As the soft lights were once more renewed, Gard started, so vividly had he reconstructed the scene as he had last looked upon it, with that hasty yet detailed scrutiny of the stage manager. He was almost surprised to find the great damask-covered easy chair untenanted, and order restored to the length and breadth of the library table. Involuntarily his eyes sought the wall behind the desk, where the panoply of ancient arms glinted somberly, then scanned the polished surface of the wood in search of what? - of the stiletto that was a foil in miniature. Somehow, though he knew that it, along with other relics of that dreadful passing, were in charge of the officials of the law, he had expected to see it there. Something of the impermanence of life and the indifferent, soulless permanence of things, flashed through his mind. "Art and art alone, enduring, stays to us," he quoted the words aloud unconsciously. "The bust outlasts the throne, the coin - Tiberius." His eyes were fixed upon the picture, which, though thrown in no relief by the unlighted globes above it, yet in its very obscurity, dominated the room with its all but unseen presence.

"Oh, no, not that alone," Teddy Mahr objected. "Don't you think we live on, in what we have done, in what we have been, in what we desire to do?"

Gard was silent. The words seemed irony. "I believe," he said slowly, "that the end is not yet. I believe that we are each accountable for our individual being. I believe that every one of us is his brother's keeper." He was silent. His own short, newly evolved credo, surprised him.

Teddy crossed to the great armchair, and laid his hand on it reverently.

"It was here his Fate found him," he said with quiet self-control. "Where will Fate find me - or you - I wonder?"

"Fate *has* found me," said Gard. "Death isn't the only thing that Fate means, but Life also; and it's of Life I came to speak to you - as well as the Past, that we must realize *is* - the Past. Of course, you know what has been learned - something about what happened here. Now, I want to tell you of my plans. I want, if possible, to keep things quiet - Oh, it's only comparatively speaking - but we can avoid a great deal of publicity, if you will let me handle the matter. It's for your sake, and I'm sure your father would desire it - and - pardon me, if I presume on grounds I'm not supposed to know anything of - but for Dorothy's, too. Dorothy may have to face bereavement too. Publicity, details, the nine days' wonder - it's all unpleasant, distressing. I have arranged to see the District Attorney to-morrow night. He can, if he will, materially aid us. This poor insane woman has delusions that it would be painful for you to even know. It would certainly be most unfortunate if she were tried or examined in public. I'd rather you didn't come - did not even see her at any time. Will you trust me? You have a perfect right to do otherwise, I know - but - will you believe me when I say I've given this my best thought, and I believe I am giving you the best advice?"

He stood very erect, speaking with formality, with a certainly stilted, "learned by rote" manner, very different from his usual fiery utterances.

Teddy respected his mood and bowed with courtly deference. "You were my father's friend," he said. "You were the last to be with him. I know you are giving me the wisest advice a wise man can give, and I accept it gratefully, Mr. Gard - for myself, and father and for Dorothy, too."

The older man held out his hand. Their clasp was strong and responsive. There were tears in Teddy's eyes, and he turned his head away quickly.

"Then," said Gard briskly, "it is understood. You also know and realize why I have kept the whole matter under seal. Why I have secreted this poor demented creature, have kept even you in ignorance of her whereabouts. Oh, I know I have had your consent all along; I know you have given me your complete trust long before this; but to-night I wanted your final cooperation in the hardest task of all - to acquiesce, while in ignorance, to permit matters that concern you, and you alone most truly and deeply, to be placed in the hands of others. I thank you for your faith, boy. God bless you."

Teddy saw his guest to the door, stood in the entry watching him descend to the street and his car, and turned away with a sigh. He reentered the room they had left, and stood for a moment in grave thought. He sighed again as he plunged the apartment in darkness and, leaving, locked the doors one after the other. Something, some very vital part of his existence was shut behind him forever. There were questions that he might not ask himself - there were veils he must not lift - there was a door in his heart, the door to the shrine of a dead man - it must be locked forever, if he would keep it a sanctuary.

In the hall once more, he turned toward the entrance; his thoughts again with the strong, kindly presence of the man who had just left him. He wondered why he had never realized the vast, unselfish human force in Gard. "What an indomitable soul," he said softly. "I must have been very blind."

*   *   *   *   *

Ethel Watts Mumford

XV

The following day found Marcus Gard at the usual morning hour in conference with Dorothy. The girl was radiant. The nurses had reported a splendid sleep and a calm awakening. She had been allowed a moment with her mother, whose voice was no longer faint, but was regaining its old vibrant quality.

The doctor entered smiling and grasped Gard's extended hand.

"You said it," he laughed. "Whatever it was, you said it, all right. Mrs. Marteen slept like a child, and there's color in her face to-day. See if you can do as well again. I'll give you five minutes - no, ten."

Preceded by the doctor, he once more found his way through the velvet-hushed corridors to the softly lighted bedroom, where lay the woman who had absorbed his every thought. Her eyes, as they met his, were bright with anxiety, and her glance at the doctor was almost resentful. But it was not part of the physician's plan to interfere with any confidence that might relieve the patient's mind. With a casual nod to Mrs. Marteen, he called to the nurse and led her from the room, his finger rapidly tapping the sick-room chart, as if medical directions were first in his mind.

Left alone, Gard approached the bed, and in answer to the unspoken question in her eyes, fumbled in his pocket and brought forth the thin packets of letters and the folded yellow cheques. One by one he laid them where her hands could touch them. He dared not look at her. He felt that her newly awakened soul was staring from her eyes at the mute evidence of a degrading past.

A moment passed in silence that seemed a year of pain; then, without a sob, without a sigh, she slowly handed him a bundle of papers, withholding them only a moment as she verified the count; then, with a slight movement she indicated the fireplace. He crossed to it and placed the papers on the coals, where they flared a moment, casting wavering shadows about the silent room, and died to black wisps. Again and again he made the short journey from the bed to the grate; each time she verified the contents of the envelopes before delivering them to his hand.

Last of all the two yellow cheques crisped to ashes. He stood looking down upon them as they dropped and collapsed into cinders, and from their ashes rose the phoenix of happiness. A glow of joyful relief lighted his spirit. There, in those dead ashes, lay a dead past - a past that might have been the black future, but was now relinquished forever, voluntarily - gone - gone! He realized a supreme moment, a turning point. Fate looked him in the eyes.

He turned, and saw a face transfigured. There was a light in Mrs. Marteen's eyes that matched the glow in his own heart. Very reverently he raised her hand and kissed it; two sudden tears fell hot upon her cheeks and her lips quivered.

He had never seen her show emotion, and it went to his heart. He saw her gaze at her hands with dilating eyes, and divined before she spoke the question she whispered:

"Who killed Victor Mahr?"

He bent above her gravely. "His wife. The wife he had cruelly wronged - his wife, who escaped at last from an asylum. She is quite mad - now. She is in our hands, and to-night, at eleven o'clock, the district attorney will be at my house to see her and have the evidence laid before him - to save Teddy," he added quickly.

She looked at him wildly. "His wife - the wife that I - "

He took her hand quickly. He feared to hear the words that he knew she was about to say.

"Yes," he nodded. "Yes - she killed him."

Mrs. Marteen sank slowly back upon her pillows and lay with closed eyes. A heavy pulse beat in the arteries at her throat, and a scarlet spot burned on either cheek.

"Nemesis," she murmured. "Nemesis." She lay still for a moment. "Thank God!" she said at length, and let her hands fall relaxed upon the counterpane. She seemed as if asleep but for the quick intake of her breath.

Gard gazed upon her with infinite tenderness, yet with sudden bitter consciousness of the isolation of each individual soul. She was remote, withdrawn. Even his eager sympathy could not reach the depths of her self-tortured heart. But now at last he knew her, a completed being. The soul was there, palpitant, awake.

The something he had so sorely missed was the living and real presence of spirit. It came over him in a wave of realization that he, too, had been unconscious of his own higher self until his love had made him feel the need of it in her. They two, from the depths of self-satisfied power, had gone blindly in their paths of self-seeking - till each had awakened the other. A strange, retarded spiritual birth.

He looked back over his long career of remorseless success with something of the self-horror he had read in her eyes as he had placed the incriminating papers in her frail hands. And as she had cast contamination from her, so he promised himself he would thrust predatory greed from his own life. They were both born anew. They would both be true to their own souls.

*   *   *   *   *

Ethel Watts Mumford

XVI

The softened electric light suffused a glamour of glowing color over the rich brocade of the walls of Marcus Gard's library, catching a glint here and there on iridescent plaques, or a mellow high light on the luscious patine of an antique bronze. The stillness, so characteristic of the place, seemed to isolate it from the whole world, save when a distant bell musically announced the hour.

Brencherly sat facing his employer, respecting his anxious silence, while they waited the coming of the district attorney, to whose clemency they must appeal - surely common humanity would counsel protective measures, secrecy, in the proceeding of the law. The links in the chain of evidence were now complete, but more than diplomacy would be required in order to bring about the legal closing of the affair without precipitating a scandal. Gard's own hasty actions led back to his fear for Mrs. Marteen, that in turn involved the cause of that suspicion. To convince the newsmongers that the crime was one of an almost accidental nature, he felt would be easy. An escaped lunatic had committed the murder. That revenge lay behind the insane act would be hidden. If necessary, the authorities of the asylum could be silenced with a golden gag - but the law?

Neither of the two men, waiting in the silent house, underestimated the importance of the coming interview.

The night was already far spent, and the expected visitor still delayed. At length the pale secretary appeared at the door to announce his coming.

Gard rose from his seat, and extended a welcoming hand to gray-haired, sharp-featured District Attorney Field.

Brencherly bowed with awkward diffidence.

Gard's manner was ease and cordiality itself, but his heart misgave him. So much depended upon the outcome of this meeting. He would not let himself dwell upon its possibilities, but faced the situation with grim determination.

"Well, Field," he said genially, "let me thank you for coming. You are tired, I know. I'm greatly indebted to you, but I'm coming straight to the point. The fact is, we," and he swept an including gesture toward his companion, "have the whole story of Victor Mahr's death. Brencherly is a detective in my personal employ." Field bowed and turned again to his host. "The person of the murderer is in our care," Gard continued. "But before we make this public - before we draw in the authorities, there are things to be considered."

He paused a moment. The district attorney's eyes had snapped with surprise.

"You don't mean to tell me," he said slowly, "that you

have the key to that mystery! Have you turned detective, Mr. Gard? Well, nothing surprises me any more. What was the motive? You've learned that, too, I suppose?"

"Insanity," said Gard shortly.

"Revenge," said the detective.

"Suppose," said Gard, "a crime were committed by a totally irresponsible person, would it be possible, once that fact was thoroughly established, to keep investigation from that person; to conduct the matter so quietly that publicity, which would crush the happiness of innocent persons, might be avoided?"

"It might," said the lawyer, "but there would have to be very good and sufficient reasons. Let's have the facts, Mr. Gard. An insane person, I take it, killed Mahr. Who?"

"His wife." Gard had risen and stood towering above the others, his face set and hard as if carved in flint.

Field instinctively recoiled. "His wife!" he exclaimed. "Why, man alive, *you* are the madman. His wife died years ago."

"No," said Gard. "Teddy Mahr's mother died. His wife is living, and is in that next room."

"What's the meaning of this?" Field demanded.

"A pretty plain meaning," Gard rejoined. "The woman escaped from the asylum where she was confined. According to her own story, she had kept track of her husband from the newspapers. Mahr couldn't divorce her, but he married again, secure in his belief that his first marriage would never be discovered. Mad as she was, she knew the situation, and she planned revenge. Dr. Malky, of the Ottawa Asylum, is here. We sent for him. The woman has been recognized by Mahr's butler as the one he admitted. There is no possible doubt. And her own confession, while it is incomplete in some respects, is nevertheless undoubtedly true.

"But, Field, this woman is hopelessly demented. There is nothing that can be done for her. She must be returned to the institution. I want to keep the knowledge of her identity from Mahr's son. Why poison the whole of his young life; why wreck his trust in his father? Convince yourself in every way, Mr. Field, but the part of mercy is a conspiracy of silence. Let it be known that an escaped lunatic did the killing - a certain unknown Mrs. Welles - and let Brencherly give the reporters all they want. For them it's a good story, anyway - such facts as these, for instance: he happened by in time to see an attack upon another woman on a bench opposite Mahr's house, and to hear her boast of her acts. But I ask as a personal favor that the scandal be avoided. Brencherly, tell what happened."

The detective looked up. "There was an old story - our office had had it - that Mahr was a bigamist. In searching for a motive for the crime, I hit on that. I had all our data on the subject sent up to me. I found that our informant stated that Mahr had a wife in an asylum somewhere. That gave me a suspicion. I found from headquarters that there were two escapes reported, and one was a woman. She had broken out of a private institution in Ottawa. I got word from there that her bills had been paid by a lawyer here - Twickenbaur. I already knew that he was Mr. Mahr's confidential lawyer. But all this I looked up later, after I'd found the woman. You see, Mr. Gard is employing me on another matter, and after he returned from Washington, I gave my report to him here.

"Then I went over to Mahr's house. I had a curiosity to go over the ground. It was quite late at night, and I was standing in the dark, looking over the location of the windows, when I saw a woman acting strangely. She was threatening and talking loudly, crying out that she had a right to kill him. I sneaked up behind just in time to stop her attack on another woman who was seated on the same bench, and who seemed too ill to defend herself. Well, sir, I had to give her three hypos before I could take her along. Then I got her to my rooms, and when she came around, she told me the story. Of course, sir, you mustn't expect any coherent narrative, though she is circumstantial enough. Then I brought over the butler, and he identified her at once. Mr. Gard advised me not to notify the police until he had seen you. We got the doctor from the asylum here as quickly as possible. He's with her in there now."

The attorney sat silent a moment, nodding his head slowly. "I'll see her, Gard," he said at length. "This is a strange story," he added, as Brencherly disappeared into the anteroom.

Field's eyes rested on Gard's face with keen questioning, but he said nothing, for the door opened, admitting the black-clad figure of a middle-aged woman, escorted by a trained nurse and a heavily built man of professional aspect.

" This is - " Field asked, as his glance took in every

detail of the woman's appearance.

"Mrs. Welles, as she is known to us," the doctor answered; "but she used to tell us that that was her maiden name, and she married a man named Mahr. We didn't pay much attention to what she said, of course, but she was forever begging old newspapers and pointing out any paragraphs about Mr. Victor Mahr, saying she was his wife."

Field gazed at the ghastly pallor of the woman's face, the maze of wrinkles and the twinkling brightness of her shifting eyes, as she stood staring about her unconcernedly. Her glance happened upon Brencherly. Her lips began to twitch and her hands to make signals, as if anxious to attract his attention. She writhed toward him.

"Young man," she whispered audibly, "they've got me - I knew they would. Even you could not keep me so hidden they couldn't find me." She jerked an accusing thumb over her shoulder at the corpulent bulk of her erstwhile jailer. "They've been trying to make me tell how I got out; but I won't tell. I may want to do it again, you see, and you won't tell."

"But," said Brencherly soothingly, "you don't want to get out now, you know. You've no reason to want to get out."

She nodded, as if considering his statement seriously.

"Of course, since I've got Victor out of the way, I don't much care. And I had awful trouble to steal enough money to get about with. Why, I had to pick ever so many pockets, and I do hate touching people; you

Ethel Watts Mumford

never can tell what germs they may have." She shook out her rusty black skirt as if to detach any possible contagion.

"But, why," the incisive voice of the attorney inquired, "did you want to kill Victor Mahr?"

"Why?" she screamed, her body suddenly stiffening. "Suppose you were his wife, and he locked you up in places, and made people call you Mrs. Welles, while he went swelling around everywhere, and making millions! What'd you do? And besides, it wasn't only *that*, you see. *I* knew, being his wife, that he was a devil - oh, yes, he was; you needn't look as if you didn't believe it. But I soon learned that when I said I was 'Mrs. Victor Mahr' in the places he put me into, they laughed at me, the way they do at my roommate, who says she's a sideboard and wants to hold a tea-set."

"Tell these gentlemen how cleverly you traced him," suggested Brencherly.

"Oh, I knew where he lived and what he was doing well enough." She bridled with conscious conceit; "I read the papers and I had it all written down. So when I got out and stole the money, I knew just where to go. But he's foxy, too. I knew I'd have to *make* him see me. So I stole some of the doctor's letterhead paper, and I wrote on it, 'Important news from the Institution' - that's what he likes to call his boarding house - an institution." She laughed. "It worked!" she went on as she regained her breath. "I just sent that message, and they let me go right in. 'Well, what is it - what is it?' Victor said, just like that." Her tones of mimicry were ghastly. She paused a moment, then broke out:

"Now you won't believe it, but I hadn't the slightest idea what I was going to kill him with when I went in there - I really didn't. The doctor will tell you himself that I'm awfully forgetful. But there, spread out before him, he had a whole collection of weapons, just as if he should say, 'Mamie, which'll you have?' I couldn't believe my eyes; so I said first thing, 'Why, you were expecting me!' He heard my voice, and his eyes opened wide; and I thought: 'If I don't do it now, he'll raise the house.' So I grabbed the big pistol and hit him! I'm telling you gentlemen all this, because I don't want anyone else to get the credit. There was a woman I met on a bench, and I just was sure she was going to take all the credit, but I told her that was *my* business. I hate people who think they can do everything. There's a woman across my hall who says she can make stars - " She broke off abruptly as for the first time she became aware of Gard's presence in the room. "Why, there you are!" she exclaimed delightedly. "Now, that's good! You can tell these people what *you* found."

"But Mr. Mahr was stabbed, Mrs. Welles," Gard interrupted. "You said you struck him with a pistol."

"Oh, I did *that* afterward." She took up the thread of her narrative. "I selected the place very carefully, and pushed the knife way in tight. I hate the sight of blood, and I sort of thought that'd stop it, and it did. Then, dear me, I had a scare. There's a picture in that room as live as life, and I looked up, and saw it looking at me. So I started to run out, but somebody was coming, so in the little room off the big one I got behind a curtain. Then this gentleman went through the room where I was, and into the room where *he* was. But he shut the door, and I couldn't see what he thought of it. After a while he came out and said 'good-night' to me, though

Ethel Watts Mumford

how he knew I was there I can't guess. So I waited a very long time, till everything was quiet, and then I went back and sat with him. It did me good just to sit and look at him; and every little while I'd lift his coat to see if the little sword was still there. The room was awful messy, and I tidied it up a bit. Then when dawn about came, I got up and walked out. I had a sort of idea of getting back to the institution without saying anything, because I was afraid they'd punish me."

"Why did you rob Mr. Mahr?" asked Mr. Field.

"Rob nothing!" she retorted.

"But his jewels, his watch," the attorney continued, his eyes riveted on her face with compelling earnestness. The woman gave an inarticulate growl. "But," interposed Brencherly, "I found his wallet in your package." He took from his pocket a worn and battered leather pocketbook and held it toward her.

"Oh," she answered indifferently, "I just took it for a souvenir. In fact, I came back for it - last thing."

Brencherly shrugged his shoulders expressively. Gard sat far back in his chair, his face in shadow.

"How long has it been, Mrs. Welles, since you - accomplished your purpose?" he asked slowly.

"You know as well as I do," she cried angrily.

"You were there. It was yesterday - no, the day before."

"It was just a week ago we found her," Brencherly said

in a low voice. "I had to look up everything and verify everything."

"You don't think I did it?" she burst out angrily. "Well, I'll prove it. I tell you I did, and I thought it all out carefully, although the doctor says I can't think connectedly. I'll show him." She fumbled in the breast of her dress for a moment, and brought out her cherished handful of newspaper clippings, which she cast triumphantly upon the table. "There's all about him from the papers, and a picture of the house. Why, I'd 'a' been a fool not to find him, and I had to. Oh, yes, I suppose, as the doctor says, I'm queer; but I wasn't when he first began sending me away - no, indeed. I wasn't good enough for him, that was all; and I was far from home, and hadn't a friend, and he had money. Oh, he was clever - but he's the devil. He used to file his horns off so people wouldn't see, but I know. So, I'll tell you everything, except how I got away. There's somebody else I may want to find." She glanced with infinite cunning at Brencherly, and began her finger signals as if practicing a dumb alphabet of which he alone knew the key.

"Where did you receive her from, Doctor?" Field asked.

"From Ogdensburg, sir. Before that they told me she was found wandering, and put under observation in Troy. All I knew was that somebody wanted her kept in a private institution. She'd always been in one, I fancy."

There was a pause as Field seemed lost in thought. Then he turned to Gard.

"May I ask you to clear one point?" he asked "You gave evidence that he was alive when you entered the room. According to her story - "

"I lied," said Gard, his pale face suffused with color. "I had to - I was most urgently needed in Washington. I would have been detained, perhaps prevented altogether from leaving. Who knows - I might even have been accused. I plead guilty of suppressing the facts."

There was silence in the room. The attorney's eyes were turned upon the self-confessed perjurer. In them was a question. Gard met their gaze gravely, without flinching. Field nodded slowly.

"You're right; publicity can only harm," he said at last. "We will see what can be done. I'll take the proper steps. It can be done legally and verified by the other witnesses. The butler identifies her, you say. It's a curious case of retribution. I can't help imagining Mahr's feelings when he recognized her voice. Is your patient at all dangerous otherwise?" He addressed himself to the nurse.

"No," she answered. "We've never seen it. Irritable, of course, but not vicious. I can't imagine her doing such a thing. But you never can tell, sir - not with this sort."

Field again addressed Gard, whose admission seemed to have exhausted him. "And the son - knows nothing?"

"Nothing," answered Gard. "He worships his father's memory. He is engaged, also, to - a very dear little friend of mine - the child of an old colleague. I want to shield them - both."

"I understand." He nodded his head slowly, lost in thought.

The woman, childishly interested in the grotesque inkwells on the table, stepped forward and raised one curiously. Her bony hands, of almost transparent thinness, seemed hardly able to sustain the weight of the cast bronze. It was hard to believe such a birdlike claw capable of delivering a stunning blow, or forcibly wielding the deadly knife. She babbled for a moment in a gentle, not unpleasant voice, while they watched her, fascinated.

"She's that way most of the time," said the nurse softly. "Just like a ten-year-old girl - plays with dolls, sir, all day long."

Suddenly her expression changed. Over her smiling wrinkles crept the whiteness of death. Her eyes seemed to start from her head, her lips drew back, while her fingers tightened convulsively on the metal inkstand. The nurse, with an exclamation, stepped forward and caught her.

There was a gleam of such maniacal fury in the woman's face that Mr. Field shuddered. "Hardly a safe child to trust even with a doll," he said. "I fancy the recital has excited her. Hadn't you better take her away and keep her quiet? And don't let anyone unauthorized by Mr. Gard or myself have access to her. It will not be wise to allow her delusion that she was the wife of Victor Mahr to become known - you understand?"

Mr. Gard rose stiffly. "I will assume the expense of her

care in future. Let her have every comfort your institution affords, Dr. Malky. I will see you to-morrow."

"Thank you, sir." The physician bowed. "Good night. Come, Mrs. Welles."

Obediently the withered little woman turned and suffered herself to be led away.

As the door closed, Field came forward and grasped Gard's hand warmly. "It is necessary for the general good," he said, his kindly face grown grave, "that this matter be kept as quiet as possible. Believe me, I understand, old friend; and, as always, I admire you."

Gard's weary face relaxed its strain. "Thanks," he said hoarsely. "We can safely trust the press to Brencherly. He," and he smiled wanly, "deserves great credit for his work. I'm thinking, Field, I need that young man in my business."

Field nodded. "I was thinking I needed him in mine; but yours is the prior claim. And now I'm off. Mr. Brencherly, can I set you down anywhere?"

Confusedly the young man accepted the offer, hesitated and blushed as he held out his hand. "May I?"

Gard read the good-will in his face, the congratulation in the tone, and grasped the extended hand with a warm feeling of friendly regard.

"Good-night - and, thank you both," he said.

*   *   *   *   *

XVII

Spring had come. The silvery air was soft with promises of leaf and bud. Invitation to Festival and Adventure was in the gold-flecked sunlight. Nature stood on tiptoe, ready for carnival, waiting for the opening measures of the ecstatic music of life's renewal.

The remote stillness of the great library had given place to the faint sounds of the vernal world. A robin preened himself at an open casement, cast a calculating eye at the priceless art treasures of the place, scorned them as useless for his needs, and fluttered away to an antique marble bench in the walled garden, wherefrom he might watch for worms, or hop to the Greek sarcophagus and take a bath in accumulated rainwater.

Marcus Gard, outwardly his determined, unbending self again, sat before his laden table, slave as ever to his tasks. Nine strokes chimed from the Gothic clock in the hall; already his busy day had begun.

Denning entered unannounced, as was his special privilege, and stood for a moment in silence, looking at his friend. Gard acknowledged his presence with a cordial nod, and continued to glance over and sign the typewritten notes before him. At last he put down his pen and settled back in his chair.

Ethel Watts Mumford

"Well, old friend, how goes it?" he inquired, smiling.

Denning nodded. "Fine, thank you. I thought I'd find you here. I was in consultation with Langley last night, and we have decided we are in a position now to go ahead as we first planned over a year ago. The opposition in Washington has been deflected. Besides, Langley dug up a point of law."

Gard rose and crossed to Denning. His manner was quietly conversational, and he twirled his *pince-nez* absently.

"My dear man," he said slowly, "you will have to adjust yourself to a shock. We will stick to the understanding as expressed in our interviews of last February, whether Mr. Langley has dug up a point of law or not. In short, Denning, we are not in future doing business in the old way."

"But you don't understand," gasped the other. "Langley says that it lets us completely out. They can't attack us under that ruling - can't you see?"

"Quite so - yes. I can imagine the situation perfectly. But we entered into certain obligations - understandings, if you will - and we are going to live up to them, whether we could climb out of them or not."

Denning sat down heavily.

"Well, I'll be - Why, it's no different from our position in the river franchise matter, not in the least - and we did pretty well with that, as you know."

Gard nodded. " Yes, we are practically in the same

position, as you say. The position is the same - but *we* are different. I suppose you've heard a number of adages concerning the irresponsibility of corporations? Well, we are going to change all that. I fancy you have already noticed a different method in our mercantile madness, and you will notice it still more in the future."

Denning pulled his mustache violently, a token with him of complete bewilderment.

"H'm - er - exactly," he murmured. "Of course, if that's the way you feel now - and you have your reasons, I suppose - I'll call Langley up. He'll be horribly disappointed, though. He's pluming himself on landing this quick getaway for you. He's been staking out the whole plan."

Gard chuckled. "Do you remember, Denning, how hard you worked to make me go to Washington - and how my 'duty to our stockholders' was your favorite weapon? Where has all that noble enthusiasm gone - eh?"

Denning blushed. "But we were in a very dangerous hole. Things are different now."

"Yes," said Gard with finality, "they are - don't forget it."

"Well," and Denning rose, discomfited, "I'm going. Three o'clock, Gard, the directors' meeting. I'll see you then."

He shook hands and turned to the door, paused, turned again as if to reopen the subject, checked himself and went out.

As the door closed Gard chuckled. "I bet he's cracking his skull to find out my game," he thought with amusement. "By the time he reaches the office, he'll have worked it out that I'm more far-sighted than the rest of them, and am making character; that I'm trying to do business by the Ten Commandments will never occur to him." He returned to the table and resumed his task, paused and sat gazing absently at the contorted inkwells.

His secretary entered quietly, a sheaf of letters in his hand.

"Saunders," said Marcus Gard, not raising his eyes from their absorbed contemplation, "did you ever let yourself imagine how hard it is to do business in a strictly honest manner, when the whole world seems to have lost the habit - if it ever *had* the habit?"

Saunders looked puzzled. "I don't know, sir. Mr. Mahr is in the hall and wants to see you," he added, glad to change the subject.

"Is he? Good. Tell him to come in." Gard rose with cordial welcome as Teddy entered.

There was an air of responsibility about the younger man, calmness, observation and concentration, very different from his former light-hearted, easy-mannered boyishness. Gard's greeting was affectionate. "Well, boy, what brings you out so early? Taking your responsibilities seriously? And in what can I help you?"

Teddy blushed. "Mr. Gard," he said, hurrying his words with embarrassment, "I wish you'd let me *give* you the Vandyke - please do. I don't want to *sell* it to you. Duveen's men are bringing it over to you this morning; they are on their way now. I want you to have it. I - I - " He looked up and gazed frankly in the older man's face, unashamed of the mist of tears that blinded him. "I know father would want you to have it. And I know, Mr. Gard, what you did to shield his memory. If you hadn't gone to Field - if you hadn't taken the matter in charge - " He choked and broke off. "I don't *know* anything - but you handled the situation as I could not. Please - won't you take the Vandyke?"

Gard's hand fell on the boy's shoulder with impressive kindliness. "No," he said quietly, "I can't do that, much as I appreciate your wanting to give it to me. I have a sentiment, a feeling about that picture. It isn't the collector's passion - I want it to remind me daily of certain things, things that you'd think I'd want to forget - but not I. I want that picture 'In Memoriam' - that's why I asked you to let me have it; and I want it by purchase. Don't question my decision any more, Teddy. You'll find a cheque at your office, that's all." He turned and indicated a space on the velvet-hung wall, where a reflector and electric lights had been installed. "It's to hang there, Teddy, where I can see it as I sit. It is to dominate my life - how much you can never guess. Will you stay with me now, and help me to receive it?"

Teddy was obviously disappointed. "I can't - I'm sorry. I ought to be at the office now; but I did so want to make one last appeal to you. Anyway, Mr. Gard, your cheque will go to enrich the Metropolitan purchase fund."

Ethel Watts Mumford

"That's no concern of mine," Gard laughed. "You can't make me the donor, you know. How is Dorothy - to change the subject!"

"What she always is," the boy beamed, "the best and sweetest. My, but I'm glad she is back! And Mrs. Marteen, she's herself again. You've seen them, of course?"

Gard nodded. "I met them at the train last night. Yes - she is - herself."

"She had an awful close call!" Teddy exclaimed, his face grown grave.

There was reminiscent silence for a moment. With an active swing of his athletic body, Dorothy's adorer collected his hat, gloves and cane in one sweep, spun on his heel with gleeful ease, smiled his sudden sunny smile, and waved a quick good-by.

*   *   *   *   *

XVIII

Teddy Mahr paused for a moment before descending to the street. He was honestly disappointed. He had hoped with all his heart to overcome Gard's opposition. Not that he was over anxious to pay, in some degree, the debt of gratitude that he owed - he had come to regard his benefactor as a being so near and dear to him that there was no question of the ethics of giving and taking, but he had longed to give himself the keen pleasure of bestowing something that his friend really wanted. There was just one more chance of achieving his purpose - the intervention of Dorothy; her caprices Gard never denied. If he could only induce Dorothy - Early as it was he determined to intreat her intercession.

Walking briskly for a few blocks, he entered an hotel and sought the telephone booth. The wide awake voice that answered him was very unlike the sweet and sleepy drawls of protest his matutinal ringings were wont to call forth when Dorothy had been a gay and frivolous debutante. The enforced quiet of her mother's prolonged illness, and the sojourn in the retirement of a hill sanitarium, had made of her a very different creature from the gaudy little night-bird of yore. The experiences through which she had passed, their anxiety and pain, had left her nature sweetened and deepened; had given her new sympathies and understandings. Now her laugh was just as clear - but its ring of light coquetry was gone.

"Of course, I'll take a walk with you," came her answer, - "if you'll stop for me. I'm quite a pedestrian, you know. I *had* to take some sort of a cure in sheer self-defense, up there in the wilds, so I decided on fresh air - and now it's a habit. I'll be ready."

Teddy walked rapidly, his heart singing. He had quite forgotten his errand in the anticipated joy of seeing her. If he thought at all of the painting, it was an unformulated regret that no living artist could do Dorothy justice, or ever hope to transfer to canvas any true semblance of her many perfections.

She joined him in the hallway of her home, called back a last happy good-by to her mother, and passed with him into the silver and crystal morning light. She was simply dressed in a dark tailor suit, with a little hat and sensible shoes - a very different silhouette from that of the girl who left her room only in time to keep her luncheon appointments. He looked at her with approval and laughed happily.

"Hello, Country! - how are the cows to-day?"

"Fine," she answered. "All boiled and sterilized, milked by electricity, manicured by steam and dehorned by absent treatment, sir, she said - sir, she said."

"May I go with you into your highly sanitary barnyard, my pretty maid?" he asked seriously.

"Not unless you take a bath in carbolic solution, are

vaccinated twice, and wear a surgeon's uniform, sir, she said."

"But, I'm going to marry you, my pretty maid." The words were out before he could check them. He blushed furiously. To propose in a nursery rhyme was something that shocked his sense of fitness. He was amazed to find that he meant what he said in just the very way he had said it.

But Dorothy took his answer as part of their early morning springtime madness.

"Nobody asked you to be farm inspector, sir, she said," she replied promptly.

But he was silent. His own words had choked him completely. She looked at him quickly, but his head was turned away. Her own heart began to beat nervously. She felt the magnetic current of his emotion vibrating through her being. Her eyes opened wide in wonder. She had for so long accustomed herself to the idea that Teddy was her own peculiar property, and that, of course, she intended to marry him, that but for his half-distressed perturbation, she would have thought no more of the momentous "Yes" than of voicing some long-formed opinion. Now his throbbing excitement had become contagious. She found herself fluttering and tongue-tied. Though she realized suddenly that their ridiculous child's-play had turned to earnest, she could not find word or look to ease the strain. They walked on in silence, step for step, in a sort of mechanical rhythmic physical understanding. Suddenly he spoke.

"Dolly, I wish you'd punch old Marcus!"

Ethel Watts Mumford

The remark was so unexpected that Dorothy slipped a beat in her step and shuffled quickly to fall in tune.

"Good Gracious! - what for?" Her surprise was unfeigned.

" Because he won't let me give him the Heim Vandyke - wants to buy it, insists on buying it. Asked me to let him have it - and then won't accept it. Now, do me a favor, will you? You *make* him take it. You're the only person who can boss him - and he likes to have you do it. Will you see him to-day, and fix it?"

"Well of all! - Why, *I* can't make him do anything he doesn't want to do. Of course, he ought to take it, if you want to give it to him; but I really don't see - I wonder - " She meditated for a full block in silence. "I'm going to lunch with him and Miss Gard and Mother. If I can, I'll - no, I *can't*. It's none of my business. It's up to you. How can I say - 'You ought to do what Teddy says'? He'd tell me I was an impertinent little girl, and that he knew how he wanted to deal with little boys without being told by their desk-mates."

Teddy scowled. He wanted to get back to the barnyard he had left so abruptly, impelled by his new and unaccountable fright. But having hitched himself to his new subject of conversation, he felt somehow compelled to drag at it. It was up-hill work. To be sure, he had come to Dorothy for the purpose of soliciting her help, but Gard and Vandyke had both lost interest. Against his will he kept on talking.

"Well, I've done everything I can to make him see my point of view. I've told him I owe it to him; that Father would want him to have it; that I'll give his money away if he sends it; that I've already shipped the thing to him; that I don't want it; that it's unbecoming to my house - he won't listen. Just says he's sent his cheque and we'll please change the subject."

"Well, you don't have to *cash* his cheque, do you?" she inquired gravely.

"I know that," Teddy scoffed. "But if I don't, he'll send it in my name, in cash, to some charity, and that'll be all the same in the final addition. He's so confoundedly resourceful, you can't think around him."

"No, you can't," she agreed. "That's one of the wonderful things about him. He thinks in his own terms, in terms of you or me, or the janitor, or the President. He isn't just himself, he's everybody."

"He isn't thinking in terms of *me*," Teddy complained.

She shook her head. "No," she smiled wisely, "he's thinking in terms of himself, this time, and we aren't big enough to see that, too, and understand."

They had reached the entrance to the Park and crossed the already crowded Plaza to its quieter walks. The tender greens of new grass greeted them, and drifts of pink and yellow vaporous color that seemed to overhang and envelop every branch of tree and shrub, like faint spirits of flower and leaf, clustering about and striving to enter the clefts of gray bark, that they might become embodied in tangible and fragile beauty. Sweet pungent smells of damp earth rose to their nostrils, - fragrance of reviving things, of stirring sap, of diligent seeds moling their way to light and air. Mists shifted by softly, now gray, now rainbow-hued,

Ethel Watts Mumford

now trailing on the grass, now sifting slowly through reluctant branches that strove to retain them.

Dorothy sighed happily. The restraint that had troubled them both slowly metamorphosed itself into a tender, dreamy content. Why ask anything of fate? Why crystallize with a word the cloudland perfection of the mirage in which they walked? They were content, happy with the vernal joy of young things in harmony with all the world of spring. They were silent now - unconscious, and one with the heart of life, as were Adam and Eve in the great garden of Eternal Spring - isolated, alone, all in all to each other, and kin with all the vibrant life about them, sentient and inanimate. For them the rainbow glowed in every drop the trailing mists scattered in their wake; for them the pale light of the sun was pure gold of dreams; every frail, courageous flower a delicate censor of fragrance. There was crooning in the tree-tops and laughter in the confidential whisper of the fountains - as if Pan's pipes had enchanted all this ruled-and-lined, sophisticated, urban *pleasaunce* into a dell in Arcady.

Teddy looked down at his companion, trudging sturdily by his side. How sweet and dear were her eyes of violet, how tender and gentle the slim curves of her mouth, how wholly lovely the contour of cheek and chin, and the curled tendrils of her moist, dark hair!

She was conscious of his gaze. She felt an impulse to take his arm - that strong, strong arm; to walk with him like that - like the old, long married couples, who come to sun themselves in the warm light of the young day, and the sight of passing lovers. A Judas tree in full blossom arrested her attention, and they came to a halt before its lavish display.

"There's nothing in the world so beautiful as natural things," she said slowly, breaking the enchanted silence.

Teddy was master of himself again. "I know," he said, "and I want to get back again to the barnyard we left so suddenly. I said something then - I want to say it over again."

It was Dorothy's turn to become frightened and confused.

"Oh," she said with an indifference she was far from feeling. "Barnyard! It's such a commonplace spot after all. Don't you like the garden better?"

But Teddy was determined. "My pretty maid," he began in a tender voice.

But she moved away suddenly down a tempting path, and, perforce, he followed her.

"I've been thinking," she said hurriedly, "about Mr. Gard. I'm sure, if he felt he was hurting your feelings, he wouldn't think *all* his own way. Now, if you want me to, I'll try and make him understand it. I'll tell him that you came to me in an awful huff - all cut up. I'm sure I can put it strongly enough."

"And I shall go to him, and complain that when I want to talk with you, you put me off - won't listen to me. I'll ask him to make you listen to reason. I'll tell him to put it to you. I'll show him that I *am* cut up, all around the heart. Perhaps he can put it to you strongly enough - "

Dorothy stopped short and wheeled around to face him.

"Oh, very well, then," she smiled, "if you are going to get someone else to do your love making for you, *I* apply for the position. Teddy Mahr, will you marry the milkmaid? - Honest and true, black and blue?"

"I will!" he cried ecstatically, and caught her in his arms.

Two wrens upon a neighboring branch, tilted forward to watch them, the business of nest building for the moment forgotten. A gray squirrel, with jerking tail and mincing gate, approached along the path. A florid policeman, wandering aimlessly in this remote arbor, stopped short, grinned, stuck his thumbs in his belt, and contemplated the picture, then wheeled about and stole out of sight in fashion most unmilitary. Across the lake the white swans glided, and two little "mandarin" ducks sidled up close to shore, regarding the moveless group of humans with bright and beady eyes.

Dorothy disengaged herself from his arms with a happy little gurgle, set her hat straight upon her tumbled hair, and glanced at the ducks.

"There," she said softly, "that's a lucky sign. In China they always send the newlyweds a pair. They are love birds; they die when separated - which means, I'm a duck."

"You are," he agreed, and kissed her again.

" Now," she said seriously, "I've found a way to clear

all difficulties."

He looked at her, troubled. "I didn't know there were any," he said anxiously. "I think your mother likes me, and I don't see - I can keep you in hats and candy; and Miss Gard is the only person who has seemed to disapprove of me."

"All wrong," she said. "I don't mean that at all. I mean about the picture. I have thought it all out while you were kissing me."

He grinned. "Did you, indeed? I'm vastly flattered, I'm sure. In that case I shall go to kissing school no later than to-morrow. However, since you work out problems in that way, I'll give you another to Q.E.D. When will the wedding be?" He folded his arms about her rapturously.

The ducks waddled up the bank; the squirrel climbed to the back of the bench; one wren captured a damaged feather from Dorothy's hat that had fallen to earth, and made off with his nest contribution.

"Now," Teddy demanded as he released her. "Did you work *that* out?"

She gasped. "If you act like that, I'll not tell you anything. I'll leave you guessing all the rest of your life."

"I expect that," he laughed. "Who am I to escape the common lot?"

She frowned. "As I was saying before you interrupted me so rudely, I have found a way to overcome the arguments and refusals of 'Old Marcus' - by the way, if he heard you call him that, he'd beat you up, and perfectly right. He isn't old, and I wish you had half his sense."

"Dolly, we are *not* married yet, and I object to unfavorable comparisons. Kindly get down to business."

"Well," she said, "I was thinking just this. We can give it to him as a wedding present - we've got him there, don't you see?"

"No, I *don't* see," he replied. "Will you kindly show me how you work that out. He'll probably want to give you a Murillo and a town house and a Cellini service, and a motor car upholstered in cloth of gold, a Florentine bust and an order on Raphael to paint your portrait. If you ask me if I see him accepting the Vandyke as a wedding present from us - I don't."

"Goose!" she said with withering scorn.

He laughed. "Oh, very well, I'm back in the barnyard, so I don't mind. Just a minute ago and you had me a duck. I've lost caste - I was a mandarin then."

"I didn't say a wedding present for *our* wedding, did I?" she inquired loftily. "Why don't you stop and think a minute. They don't teach observation in college, evidently."

Teddy was nonplussed. "You've got me," he said, his brows drawn together in a puzzled frown.

She tapped her foot impatiently. "Well, how else could we be giving him a wedding present?" she inquired.

"That's just what I don't see," he replied emphatically.

"When *he* gets married, of course - heavens! you are dense!"

Teddy was stunned. "When he - why - what nonsense! - he's a confirmed old bachelor. There! I knew you couldn't think out problems when I was kissing you. I'm glad you didn't answer my second question, if that's the way you work things out. Who in the world would he marry!"

"How would you like him for a step-father-in-law?" She looked at him with an amused smile.

"Good gracious!" he exclaimed. "Why, I never thought of that! Your mother! - Oh, by golly! that's great, that's great! Of course, of course. Here, I'll kiss you again - you can answer my second question." He embraced her with hysterical enthusiasm. "Oh, when did it happen?" he begged. "How did you know? Since when have they been engaged? My! I have been a bat! Where were my eyes? Of all the jolly luck!" he leaped from the bench and executed a triumphal war dance.

"You act just like the kids - I mean, the baby goats, up in the Bronx," she laughed. "Teddy, stop, somebody might see you, and they'd send us both to an asylum. Stop it! And besides, my step-father hasn't proposed yet."

Teddy ceased his gambols abruptly. "What in the world have you been telling me, then?" he demanded, crestfallen. "Here I've been celebrating an event that hasn't happened."

Ethel Watts Mumford

"Well, it's going to," she affirmed with an impressive nod of her head. "*I* know. Why, even Mother hasn't the slightest idea of it yet. Poor, dear Mother, she's so really humble minded, she wouldn't let herself realize how he loves her. But she leans on him, on the very thought of him. When we were away recuperating, she used to watch for his letters - like - like - I watched for yours, Teddy; and when I'd hand her one, she had such a look of calm, of rest. I've found her asleep with one crushed up in her hand. I'm sure she used to put them under her pillow at night, just as - well - just as I used to put yours, Teddy, under mine. Don't you know, that when two women are in love, they know it one from another, without a word. Of course, Mother knew all about how *I* felt, I used to catch her looking at me, oh, so wistfully - but she never dreamed that wise little daughter had guessed her secret - oh, no - mothers never realize that their little chick-children have grown to be big geese. But, *I* know, and, well, Teddy, as you know, if he doesn't ask her pretty soon, I'll go and ask him myself - and he never refuses me anything. I shall say, 'Dear old Marcus, Teddy and I wish you'd hurry up and ask Mother to marry you. We have set our hearts on picking out our own "steps." We think of being married in June, and we want it all settled.' There," she said with a radiant blush, "I've answered all your questions - have you another problem?"

*   *   *   *   *

XIX

Left alone before the empty space reserved for the masterpiece the expression on Gard's face changed. Grave and purposeful, he continued to regard the blank wall, then, turning, he caught up the desk telephone, gave Mrs. Marteen's private number and waited.

A moment later the sweet familiar voice thrilled him.

"It's I - Marcus," he said. "I am coming for you this morning. Yes, I'm taking a holiday, and I'm going to bring you back to the library to see a new acquisition of mine - that will interest you. Then you and Dorothy will lunch with Polly. Dorothy can join us at one o'clock. This is a private view - for you alone.... You will? That's good! Good-by."

Noises in the resonant hall and the opening of the great doors announced the arrival of the moving van and its precious contents, before Saunders, his eyes bulging with excitement, rushed in with the tidings of the coming of the world famous Heim Vandyke. With respectful care the great canvas was brought in, unwrapped and lifted to its chosen hanging place.

Seated in his armchair, Gard with mixed emotions watched it elevated and straightened. The pictured face smiled down at him - impersonal yet human, glowing,

Ethel Watts Mumford

vivid with color, alive with that suggestion of eternal life that art alone in its highest expression can give. Card's smile was enigmatical; his eyes were sad. His imagination pictured to him Mrs. Marteen as she had sat before him in her self-contained stateliness and announced with indifferent calm that the Vandyke had been but a ruse to gain his private ear.

Gard rose, approached the picture, and for an instant laid his fingers upon its darkened frame. The movement was that of a worshiper who makes his vow at the touch of some relic infinitely holy.

Then he returned to his seat and for some time remained wrapped in thought. These moments of introspection, of deep self-questioning, had become more and more frequent. He had made in the past few months a new and most interesting acquaintance - himself. All the years of his over-hurried, over-cultivated, ambitious life he had delved into the psychology of others. It had been his pride to divine motives, to dissect personalities, to classify and sort the brains and natures of men. Now for the first time he had turned the scalpel upon himself. He was amazed, he was shocked, almost frightened. He could not hide from himself, he was no longer blind, the searchlight of his own analysis was inexorably focused on his own sins and shortcomings - his powers misused, his strength misdirected, his weaknesses indulged, because his strength protected them. In these hours of what he had grown to grimly call his "stock taking," he had become aware of a new and all-important group of men. Where before he had reckoned values solely by capacities of brain and hand, he found now a new factor - the capacity of heart. Ideals that heretofore had borne to his mind the stamp of weakness, now showed themselves as real bulwarks of character. The men who had fallen by the wayside in the advance of his pitiless march to power, were no longer, to his eyes, types of the unfit, to be thrust aside. Some were men, indeed, who knew their own souls, and would not barter them.

In his mind a vast readjustment had taken place. Words had become bodied, the unseen was becoming the visible - Responsibility, Honesty, Fairness, Truth! they had all been words to conjure with - for use in political speeches, in interviews - because they seemed to exercise an occult influence upon the gullible public. "Law," "Peace," "Order," "The Greatest Good to the Greatest Number," he had used them all as an Indian medicine-man shakes bone rattles, and waves a cow's tail before the tribe, laughing behind his gaping mask at the servile acceptance of his prophecies. One and all these Cunjar Gods he had believed to be only bits of shell and plaited rope, had come to life - they *were* gods, real presences, real powers. He had invoked them only to deceive others - and, behold! he it was who knew not the truth.

The high tower of his heaven-grasping ambitions seemed suddenly insecure and founded upon shifting sands. The incense the sycophant world burned before him became a stench in his nostrils. The fetishes he had tossed to the crowd now faced him as real gods; and they were not to be blinded with dust, nor bought with gold. The specious and tortured verbiage of twisted law never for one moment deceived the open ears of Justice, even though it tied her hands, and her voice was the voice of condemnation. Honor - he had sold it. Faith - he had not kept it. Truth - he had distorted to fit whatever garb he had chosen for her to wear. And, withal, he had hailed himself conqueror; had placed his laurels himself upon his head, ranking all others beneath him. The clamor of the mob he had interpreted as acclaim. Now he heard above the applause the hoarse chorus of disdain and fear. It had been his pride to see men fall back and make way at the very mention of his name. Now he felt that they shrank from him - not before his greatness, but from his very contact. He had driven his fellow creatures from him, and in return, they withdrew themselves.

If they came to him fawning, they but showed their lower natures. He had not called forth the power for good, from these the necromancy of his personality had touched. He had conjured evil, he had pandered to base forces.

The realization had not come easily. His habits of thought would return and blind him as of old. He had laughed at himself; he had derided the new gods, he had disobeyed them and their strange commands - only to return crestfallen, contrite, feeling himself unworthy. He became aware that he had run a long and victorious race for a prize he had craved - only to find that the goal to which it brought him was not that of his old desires. That was but withered leaves, spattered with the blood of those who lost. He had turned from it, and now his steps sought another conquest and another reward. He must strive for a goal unseen, but more real and more worthy than the little crowns of little victories.

His somber thoughts left him refreshed, as if from a bath of deep, clear waters. His spirit felt clean and elated as it rose from the depths. It was with a smile that he pushed back his chair and rose from the table where, for a full hour, he had sat in silent self-communing. He still smiled as he entered the motor and was driven to Mrs. Marteen's.

He found her awaiting him, with outstretched hands, and the look in her eyes that he always longed for - the look he had divined rather than seen on that day of days, when the Past had been renounced and consumed. There was no embarrassment in their meeting. True, there had been daily exchange of letters during the months of her enforced exile; but they had been only friendly, surface tokens, giving no real hint of the realities beneath. But they had grown toward one another, not apart. It was as if they had never been sundered; as if all the experiences of all the intervening days had been experiences in common.

He gazed at her happily now, rejoicing in the firmness of her step, the brightness of her eyes, the healthy color of her skin. She came with him gladly at his suggestion and they drove in silence through the crowded streets and the silence was in truth, golden. At the door of the great house he descended, gave her his hand and conducted her quickly through the vast, soft-lighted hall to his own sanctum. He closed the door quietly and pressed the electric switch. Instantly the mellow lights glowed above the portrait, which throbbed in response, a glittering gem of warmth and beauty.

Mrs. Marteen's body stiffened; the color receded from her face, leaving it ashen. Her great eyes dilated.

"Do you know why it is there?" he asked at length in a whisper.

" Yes," she murmured. "We have traveled the same

road - you and I. I understand."

He took her hand and raised it to his lips. "You don't know all that this picture recalls to me - and I hope you will never know; but you and I," he said slowly, weighing his words, "are not of the breed of those who cry out with remorse. We are of those who live differently. That is the constant reminder of what *was*. I do not want to forget. I want to remember. Every time the iron enters my soul I shall know the more keenly that I have at last a soul."

Again they fell silent.

"According to the accepted code I suppose I should make a clean breast of it, even to Dorothy, and go into retirement," she said at length. "I have thought of that, too; but I cannot *feel* it. I want to be active; to be able to use myself for betterment; make of myself an example of good and not of evil. What I did was because of what I was. I am that no longer, and my expression must be of the new thing that has become me - a soul!" she said reverently.

"A soul," he repeated. "It has come to me, too. And what is left to me of life has no place for regrets. I have that which I must live up to - I *shall* live up to it."

"We have, indeed, traveled the same road; but you - have led me." She looked at him with complete comprehension.

"We will travel the new road together," he said finally, "hand in hand."

Choose from Thousands of 1stWorldLibrary Classics By

Adolphus William Ward
Aesop
Agatha Christie
Alexander Aaronsohn
Alexander Kielland
Alexandre Dumas
Alfred Gatty
Alfred Ollivant
Alice Duer Miller
Alice Turner Curtis
Alice Dunbar
Ambrose Bierce
Amelia E. Barr
Andrew Lang
Andrew McFarland Davis
Anna Sewell
Annie Besant
Annie Hamilton Donnell
Annie Payson Call
Anton Chekhov
Arnold Bennett
Arthur Conan Doyle
Arthur Ransome
Atticus
B. M. Bower
Basil King
Bayard Taylor
Ben Macomber
Booth Tarkington
Bram Stoker
C. Collodi
C. E. Orr
C. M. Ingleby
Carolyn Wells
Catherine Parr Traill
Charles A. Eastman
Charles Dickens
Charles Dudley Warner
Charles Farrar Browne
Charles Ives
Charles Kingsley
Charles Lathrop Pack
Charles Whibley
Charles Willing Beale
Charlotte M. Braeme
Charlotte M. Yonge
Clair W. Hayes
Clarence Day Jr.
Clarence E. Mulford

Clemence Housman
Confucius
Cornelis DeWitt Wilcox
Cyril Burleigh
D. H. Lawrence
Daniel Defoe
David Garnett
Don Carlos Janes
Donald Keyhole
Dorothy Kilner
Dougan Clark
E. Nesbit
E.P.Roe
E. Phillips Oppenheim
Edgar Allan Poe
Edgar Rice Burroughs
Edith Wharton
Edward J. O'Biren
John Cournos
Edwin L. Arnold
Eleanor Atkins
Elizabeth Cleghorn
Gaskell
Elizabeth Von Arnim
Ellem Key
Emily Dickinson
Erasmus W. Jones
Ernie Howard Pie
Ethel Turner
Ethel Watts Mumford
Eugenie Foa
Eugene Wood
Evelyn Everett-Green
Everard Cotes
F. J. Cross
Federick Austin Ogg
Ferdinand Ossendowski
Francis Bacon
Francis Darwin
Frances Hodgson Burnett
Frank Gee Patchin
Frank Harris
Frank Jewett Mather
Frank L. Packard
Frederick Trevor Hill
Frederick Winslow Taylor
Friedrich Kerst
Friedrich Nietzsche
Fyodor Dostoyevsky

Gabrielle E. Jackson
Garrett P. Serviss
Gaston Leroux
George Ade
Geroge Bernard Shaw
George Ebers
George Eliot
George MacDonald
George Orwell
George Tucker
George W. Cable
George Wharton James
Gertrude Atherton
Grace E. King
Grant Allen
Guillermo A. Sherwell
Gulielma Zollinger
Gustav Flaubert
H. A. Cody
H. B. Irving
H. G. Wells
H. H. Munro
H. Irving Hancock
H. Rider Haggard
H. W. C. Davis
Hamilton Wright Mabie
Hans Christian Andersen
Harold Avery
Harold McGrath
Harriet Beecher Stowe
Harry Houidini
Helent Hunt Jackson
Helen Nicolay
Hendy David Thoreau
Henrik Ibsen
Henry Adams
Henry Ford
Henry Frost
Henry James
Henry Jones Ford
Henry Seton Merriman
Henry Wadsworth
Longfellow
Henry W Longfellow
Herbert A. Giles
Herbert N. Casson
Herman Hesse
Homer
Honore De Balzac

Horace Walpole
Horatio Alger, Jr.
Howard Pyle
Howard R. Garis
Hugh Lofting
Hugh Walpole
Humphry Ward
Ian Maclaren
Israel Abrahams
J.G.Austin
J. Henri Fabre
J. M. Barrie
J. Macdonald Oxley
J. S. Knowles
J. Storer Clouston
Jack London
Jacob Abbott
James Allen
James Lane Allen
James Andrews
James Baldwin
James DeMille
James Joyce
James Oliver Curwood
James Oppenheim
James Otis
Jane Austen
Jens Peter Jacobsen
Jerome K. Jerome
John Burroughs
John F. Kennedy
John Gay
John Glasworthy
John Habberton
John Joy Bell
John Milton
John Philip Sousa
Jonathan Swift
Joseph Carey
Joseph Conrad
Joseph Jacobs
Julian Hawthrone
Julies Vernes
Justin Huntly McCarthy
Kakuzo Okakura
Kenneth Grahame
Kate Langley Bosher
L. A. Abbot
L. T. Meade
L. Frank Baum
Laura Lee Hope

Laurence Housman
Leo Tolstoy
Leonid Andreyev
Lewis Carroll
Lilian Bell
Lloyd Osbourne
Louis Tracy
Louisa May Alcott
Lucy Fitch Perkins
Lucy Maud Montgomery
Lydia Miller Middleton
Lyndon Orr
M. H. Adams
Margaret E. Sangster
Margaret Vandercook
Maria Edgeworth
Maria Thompson Daviess
Mariano Azuela
Marion Polk Angellotti
Mark Overton
Mark Twain
Mary Austin
Mary Cole
Mary Rowlandson
Mary Wollstonecraft
Shelley
Max Beerbohm
Myra Kelly
Nathaniel Hawthrone
O. F. Walton
Oscar Wilde
Owen Johnson
P.G.Wodehouse
Paul and Mable Thorn
Paul G. Tomlinson
Paul Severing
Peter B. Kyne
Plato
R. Derby Holmes
R. L. Stevenson
Rabindranath Tagore
Rahul Alvares
Ralph Waldo Emmerson
Rene Descartes
Rex E. Beach
Richard Harding Davis
Richard Jefferies
Robert Barr
Robert Frost
Robert Gordon Anderson
Robert L. Drake

Robert Lansing
Robert Michael Ballantyne
Robert W. Chambers
Rosa Nouchette Carey
Ross Kay
Rudyard Kipling
Samuel B. Allison
Samuel Hopkins Adams
Sarah Bernhardt
Selma Lagerlof
Sherwood Anderson
Sigmund Freud
Standish O'Grady
Stanley Weyman
Stella Benson
Stephen Crane
Stewart Edward White
Stijn Streuvels
Swami Abhedananda
Swami Parmananda
T. S. Ackland
The Princess Der Ling
Thomas A. Janvier
Thomas A Kempis
Thomas Anderton
Thomas Bailey Aldrich
Thomas Bulfinch
Thomas De Quincey
Thomas H. Huxley
Thomas Hardy
Thomas More
Thornton W. Burgess
U. S. Grant
Valentine Williams
Victor Appleton
Virginia Woolf
Walter Scott
Washington Irving
Wilbur Lawton
Wilkie Collins
Willa Cather
Willard F. Baker
William Makepeace
Thackeray
William W. Walter
Winston Churchill
Yei Theodora Ozaki
Young E. Allison
Zane Grey

www.ingramcontent.com/pod-product-compliance
Lightning Source LLC
Chambersburg PA
CBHW030302180626
46810CB00003B/898